D0571836

# DANCING
# ON A RAINBOW

~

## From the library of

Name_____

Address_____

_____

_____

# THE ROMANTIC NOVELS OF

# BARBARA CARTLAND

## DANCING
## ON A RAINBOW

Eaglemoss Publications Limited,
7 Cromwell Road,
London SW7 2HR

First published 1986

Set in Sabon
Made and printed in Great Britain by
Richard Clay (The Chaucer Press) Ltd,
Bungay, Suffolk

ISBN 1 85167 017 3

# Dancing on a Rainbow

The Duke of Madrescourt, an extremely dictatorial obstinate man, informs his daughter, Lady Loretta, that he has arranged for her to marry the son of *le Duc de* Sauerdun.

Loretta is horrified at the idea of having to marry a man she has never seen, and does not love, although she knows it is usual amongst the French and the British aristocrats to arrange marriages for their children.

While her father is away racing, greatly daring, she journeys with a former maid to Paris to contact her cousin Ingrid, who a few years earlier had run away from her dull, indifferent, old husband, with the attractive Marquess of Galston.

How Loretta pleads with Ingrid to help her meet Fabian de Sauerdun without him being aware who she is, so that she can persuade her father it is impossible for her to marry him; how she finds Fabian is quite different to what she expected; how she saves herself from the very unwelcome attentions of a Parisian womaniser and how she finds life in Paris is very strange and different to anything she has ever known before, is told in this fascinating new novel by Barbara Cartland.

# AUTHOR'S NOTE

In the last ten years of the 19th Century Paris became the civilised world Capital of elegant living, pleasure and artistic genius.

The Eiffel Tower, built in 1889, and the highest metal structure in the world, symbolised a turbulent century of great achievements for Paris.

Paris was growing more prosperous and more bourgeois. It was also becoming increasingly democratic despite many social injustices. The war debts had been paid off to victorious Germany ahead of schedule, and France's colonial Empire was growing fast.

The areas in the city which had been ravaged by fire and artillery had been rebuilt; the Opera House was completed and there was little to show that Paris had suffered a siege and a Civil War.

For the sophisticated searcher of pleasure, there was nowhere in the world to rival Paris. Already famous for women's fashions, for its brilliant high society life, its food and its music, from 1889 there was the added allure of the *Moulin Rouge*. The great, red wooden sails of the windmill above its entrance began to turn, and for the next decade became a mecca for those with money to spend.

Writers and the artists of the time found complete freedom in Paris. They could write, paint and live as they liked, amongst people with a passion for novelty.

There was freedom of the press; freedom to express political convictions; freedom to create and freedom to look to the future.

It was a new age which had a large number of troubles and difficulties, but which also had so much charm, vitality and colour, which combined with an abundance of pleasure, has since become known as 'La Belle Epoque'.

# CHAPTER ONE

## 1889

Lady Loretta Court patted her horse's neck before she dismounted.

"He went well today, Ben," she said to the groom who was waiting to take him to the stables.

"'E allus likes ye to ride 'im, M'Lady," Ben grinned, and she smiled at him as she walked up the steps and into the big hall.

She had just reached the top of the stairs when a footman came hurrying from a corridor to say:

"His Grace wishes to speak to you, M'Lady, and asks that you go to the Study as soon as you return."

Loretta gave a little sigh. She had been riding for two hours and she wanted to change from her riding-habit and have a bath.

However, if her father wanted her, there was nothing she could do but obey.

She went down the stairs she had already climbed and handed the footman her riding-gloves and the small whip which she never used, and almost defiantly took off her riding-hat and gave it to him as well.

Pushing her hair into place she hurried through the Hall along the wide corridor which led to her father's Study.

She wondered what he could want, and thought that if it was anything to do with her riding without a groom, which he disliked, he would undoubtedly be very long-winded about what he had to say, and it would be difficult to escape from him.

Loretta was very fond of her father, but since her mother's death she had found him extremely dictatorial.

Like many elderly men, he seldom listened to what anybody else had to say.

In his position as Lord Lieutenant of the County he had a great deal to occupy him, but he was never too busy for his only daughter.

At the same time, he had very strict ideas of propriety which Loretta found restricting as well as boring.

She opened the door of the Study and went in apprehensively.

At the same time, it struck her as it always did what a beautiful room it was.

She appreciated even more than her father did the pictures of horses which decorated the walls.

When he was young the Duke had been one of the most handsome of Queen Victoria's Lords-in-Waiting.

Now he was, in fact, in an exceedingly good humour, as he looked up from the desk at which he was writing.

There was a pile of papers in front of him, because although he had a secretary, the Duke's motto was:

"If you want anything done well, you must do it yourself!"

This resulted in his having a quite unnecessary amount of paperwork to do.

He smiled however, when he saw Loretta and thought, as he often had before, that he was fortunate to have such a lovely daughter.

It was indeed only to be expected, seeing that her mother had been without exception the most beautiful woman he had ever seen.

"You wanted me, Papa?"

"Yes, Loretta, I have something important to tell you.

I thought it would be a mistake to talk about it last night, since I was tired when I returned from the races, and I also wanted you to sleep well."

There was a worried expression in Loretta's eyes as she asked:

"What is it you want to tell me, Papa, which you could not tell me last night?"

The Duke rose from his desk and walked across the room to stand in front of a magnificently carved mantelpiece above which hung a very fine painting by Sartorius.

"When I was at Epsom yesterday," he began, "I saw my old friend the *Duc de* Sauerdun."

Because her father was speaking slowly and rather pompously, Loretta was sure that whatever he had to say was going to take a long time and she sat down in one of the armchairs.

She had often heard her father speak of the *Duc*. She knew that although they might be of different nationalities the two old gentlemen had a close bond between them in that they ran race-horses both in France and in England and often against each other.

"Did you beat the *Duc*'s horse yesterday?" Loretta asked.

"As a matter of fact *Minotaur* romped home half a length ahead of Sauerdun's horse!" the Duke said with satisfaction.

"I am glad, Papa. You must be very pleased."

"After the race was over," her father went on, as though she had not spoken, "Sauerdun and I had a drink together, and he made a suggestion which had not occurred to me before, but one which I find extremely satisfactory."

"What was that, Papa?"

She was thinking her father was taking a long time getting to the point and wondering how soon she could escape upstairs.

"I have been considering for some time, Loretta," the Duke replied, "whom you should marry, and the *Duc*'s suggestion that it should be his son seems a very satisfactory solution to the problem."

Loretta sat bolt upright and her whole body was tense.

"What . . what are you saying . . Papa?" she asked. "I do not know what you are . . talking about!"

"I am talking my dear, about your marriage, and it would give me great pleasure to give you away to the *Marquis de* Sauerdun who, on his father's death, will inherit a magnificent *Château* in the Loire Valley, as well as vast estates in Normandy, where the Sauerduns originally came from."

"But . . Papa!" Loretta exclaimed. "You cannot be serious! How can you possibly arrange my marriage with a man I have . . never even met? And you . . promised me I should have a . . Season in London."

"I know! I know!" the Duke said somewhat testily. "But quite frankly, my dear, this is too good an opportunity to miss."

Loretta got to her feet.

She was slim and not very tall, and though her father seemed to tower above her, she faced him defiantly.

"I have no intention, Papa, whatever you may say, of marrying somebody with whom I am not in love!"

"Love?" the Duke growled. "Love will come after marriage. What you have to do, as my only daughter, is to marry the right man; a man with a proper position in life and one I will choose for you."

"B . . but Papa, I have to marry him – not you!"

"I know that," the Duke said angrily, "but if you think I am going to let you marry some whipper-snapper who is impressed by your social rank, or thinks because I have no son you will inherit a great deal of money, you are very much mistaken."

"But Papa, the only men I have met at the moment are

those who live in the County and whom I have known all my life," Loretta protested.

She went on rather sadly:

"Because Mama died, I have never been to parties or Balls or anywhere else where I was likely to meet the man who might be my future husband."

"Even if you had been to Balls," the Duke answered, "you would not have been likely to meet anybody more suitable than the *Marquis* de Sauerdun."

"He may be very suitable from a social point of view," Loretta said, "but how can I know if I will be happy with him as a husband if I have never even met him?"

"You will meet him! Of course you will meet him!" the Duke replied. "I said to Sauerdun:

"'You had better bring your son to stay at Madrescourt before Royal Ascot.'

"He thought that was a good idea, and your engagement can be announced before the end of the Season."

"But, Papa, you are arranging it all! You are not giving me a chance to decide for myself whether I wish to marry the *Marquis* or whether I dislike him so much that I shall refuse to do anything of the sort."

"Refuse? What do you mean – refuse?" the Duke asked. "I have never heard such nonsense! In France, as you are well aware, Loretta, marriages are arranged. The *Duc* is quite right, and his son should not make a mistake a second time."

"A second time!" Loretta exclaimed. "What do you mean?"

"The *Marquis* was married when he was very young," her father replied. "Apparently, so Sauerdun tells me, he was infatuated with a young girl he met in Paris."

He paused before continuing:

"She came of a good family and there was no reason why the *Duc* should not agree to the marriage, it took

13

place and proved disastrous! The young people did not get on, there was no sign of an heir, and then fortunately for the *Marquis* she was involved in a carriage accident and died of her injuries."

The Duke paused, then added before his daughter could speak:

"This time Sauerdun is taking no chances. He has chosen his son's wife with the same care that he expends on his horses!"

"Horses!" Loretta cried, but the Duke continued as if she had not spoken:

"Having heard how attractive you are and knowing you are my daughter, he is determined that the marriage shall take place as soon as possible after you have met and become engaged."

"I will not do it, Papa! I know exactly what you are saying, that I have absolutely no choice as to whether I will or will not marry the *Marquis*. He will come here, and by the time he arrives you will have told most of our relatives why you have invited him."

Her voice rose as she went on:

"Then once you have said we are to be married, it will be impossible for me not to accept his proposal, if he ever makes one himself!"

As Loretta finished speaking, the Duke flew into one of his rages.

The whole household knew them well.

Because he was such a large man and, when angry, very frightening, Loretta became paler and paler as he raged at her.

He called her ungrateful, inconsiderate, selfish and unfeeling.

He said she was deliberately upsetting him when she knew quite well he was lonely and distraught after her mother's death.

He accused her of being heartless.

14

Despite every resolution she made not to let him upset her, it brought tears to her eyes.

Finally when she wished to speak he would not listen.

"You will be married to Sauerdun if I have to drag you up the aisle! I will have no more nonsense about your falling in love."

He looked at her sternly as he went on:

"You will obey me, Loretta, do you hear me? You will obey me, and that is my final word on the matter!"

He shouted at her until Loretta knew she could bear it no longer!

With a little sob she turned and ran from the room.

As she crossed the Hall and climbed the stairs to her bedroom the tears were streaming down her cheeks.

When she reached it she slammed the door behind her and pulling off her riding-jacket sat down on the bed covering her face with her hands.

"What am I to do? Oh, God, what am I to do?" she asked.

Ever since she had been old enough to read love-stories starting with '*Romeo and Juliet*' and finding her heart beat a little quicker, she had looked into the future when she herself would find love.

It was then she had been sure that one day she would meet the man of her dreams.

As she grew older he grew more and more real.

Although he was faceless she almost felt he was there beside her.

Already their thoughts had merged together and eventually he would materialise as a real man, and they would live happily ever after.

It was a child's fairy-story, but at the same time, as the years passed, it grew to be so much a part of Loretta's life.

Never a day or a night passed without she was telling herself of her love, or rather living it in her mind.

Her dream-man was always with her, climbing the Himalayas, sailing up the Amazon, being ship-wrecked on a desert island, pursued by brigands, or chased by an Arab tribe.

He always saved her, and she knew because he was with her she need never really be afraid.

Secretly she thought that when the mourning for her mother was over and she went to London, her dream-man would be waiting for her.

Perhaps at one of the big Balls given by the famous hostesses who were all friends of her father's.

Or she would meet him at the Ball which would be given for her at the family house in Park Lane.

What would be the most romantic of all, would be if she found him at Buckingham Palace in the Throne Room when with the three white Prince of Wales feathers in her hair she made her curtsy.

This would be either to her Majesty Queen Victoria, or if she was indisposed, to the beautiful Princess of Wales.

It had already been arranged that Madrescourt House in Park Lane should be open to receive Loretta and her father.

Her aunt, the Countess of Bredon, who was to chaperon her while she was in London, would also be with her.

The Countess had sent down to the country for Loretta to choose a number of attractive gowns in which she was to make her début.

They all came from the most expensive and fashionable dressmakers in Bond Street.

Loretta, while admitting they were quite appropriate for what she would be doing in London, thought they had no individuality about them.

However, as her father was extremely generous to her, she was determined when she reached London to find a number of other dresses.

They would reflect her own taste, rather than that of her aunt's which was more conventional.

Now she knew, although her father had not said as much that there would be no point in her going to London.

No reason at all except for the actual Drawing-Room at Buckingham Palace when she would be presented to the Queen.

Instead everything would be concentrated on the moment that the *Duc de* Sauerdun and his son the *Marquis* arrived, which Loretta anticipated would be at the end of May or early in June.

"I shall be deprived of the chance of meeting anyone else, especially after what I have already said to Papa," Loretta thought.

Because she was so close to her father, she knew exactly how his mind worked, and she was sure he would now make every excuse not to take her to London.

He would instead concentrate on preparing to entertain his future son-in-law in what might be termed Royal fashion.

"It is unfair .. very .. unfair!" Loretta told herself, and felt as if she was in a trap from which there was no escape.

At the same time, she was determined not to be forced into a loveless marriage which she was certain would be disastrous not only for herself but for anyone who married her.

She had to find some way to circumvent it.

It was not going to be easy – she was well aware of that – knowing what her father was like when he had made up his mind.

She was also intelligent enough to realise that the idea of her being married to the *Duc de* Sauerdun's son was a sensible one from a parental point of view.

Of course the *Marquis* was what was called 'a good

catch' and it was doubtful if there was any eligible young man in England who could match him for social position or for the wealth that the Sauerduns possessed.

Loretta had heard in the past how exceptional it was, and indeed their possessions were extolled over the whole world.

She had not listened very attentively when her father spoke of the pictures owned by the Sauerduns, she realised from what he said that they rivalled the collections in the Louvre and in the National Gallery.

But she had been impressed by the Duc's horses, and his stable was certainly larger and more successful than her father's, or perhaps than anyone else's in England.

She could understand that when *Minotaur*, her father's best race-horse, had beaten the *Duc*'s it had put him in a good humour, and following that he would have agreed to anything which might be suggested.

She could only think that the *Duc de* Sauerdun must have some special reason for arranging his son's marriage in such haste, rather than inviting her and her father to stay with them in France.

'It is so like Papa,' Loretta thought, 'to make up his mind in a hurry and insist that I should be married to a Frenchman I have never even seen, just because he likes his father and they have an interest in the same sport.'

At the same time, she knew that her father was speaking the truth when he said that French marriages were always arranged.

In the case of aristocratic families the same more or less applied in England.

"Whatever anybody else may think, I will be the exception!" Loretta told herself defiantly.

But she knew as she spoke that it was going to be very, very difficult, and she would have to be extremely clever about it.

At the same time, just as her father was always obstinate when it came to getting his own way, she could be the same.

Having changed, she went down to luncheon looking pale and subdued.

She hoped that her father would feel somewhat guilty when he realised from her silence and downcast eyes that she was distressed.

He was, however, in such a good humour at the idea of her marriage that she thought he hardly noticed her reaction.

He assumed that because he had raged at her, she would no longer oppose him.

They were alone, because the cousin who had been staying in the house for some months as a companion for Loretta, especially while her father was away at the races, had retired to bed with a cold.

The Duke spent the first part of the meal talking about the races he had attended the day before.

He described in detail how he had defeated several outstanding horses, as well as that of the *Duc de* Sauerdun.

"The day after tomorrow," he said, "I am going to Newmarket, and I am hoping I shall be as successful there as I was yesterday."

Loretta did not answer and the Duke said testily:

"Oh, for God's sake, child, stop looking as if you had lost a half-crown, and found a threepenny bit! Most girls would be jumping over the moon with joy at the idea of making such a magnificent marriage their first Season."

"But I have not had a Season, Papa!" Loretta said plaintively.

The Duke considered this for a moment. Then he said.

"Well, if that is what is troubling you, I will see what we can do. There is no point in opening the house in London and giving a Ball as we had planned."

He thought for a moment and then added:

"We will have one here when the Sauerduns are staying with us, and you had better talk to your Cousin Emily and plan a more magnificent Ball than any of those we have given in the past."

Loretta knew without his saying so, that he intended at the Ball to announce publicly her engagement to the *Marquis*.

She, however, did not say anything except:

"That sounds a very .. nice idea, Papa."

"It pleases you?" the Duke exclaimed. "Well, that is a good girl! And I will take you to London when you are presented at The Drawing Room. I think that is in the middle of May, is it not?"

"Yes, Papa."

"Right! Then we will attend a Ball or two, and watch the Polo at Ranelagh, but there will be little point in opening the house completely as we had intended. We can keep everything until after Ascot."

"Yes, Papa," Loretta agreed.

Only when luncheon was over and the Duke had hurried off to a meeting at County Hall did she change once again into her riding-habit.

Disobeying the Duke's strict instructions that she should always take a groom with her, she rode off.

On the edge of the woods about three miles from the house she knew that Christopher Willoughby would be waiting for her.

He was a young man she had known ever since she was a child, whose estate marched with the Duke's though it was very much smaller, and in her father's eyes, unimportant.

In fact, he treated it with the same lofty condescension with which he treated Christopher's father.

He might be the 5th Baronet, but was not well off and was unable to contribute much to the charitable organisations of which the Duke was a Patron.

If the Duke had been aware of how often Christopher and his daughter met each other out riding, he would have been furious.

But Christopher was the only young man Loretta knew well.

Although Christopher had been in love with her for the last three years, she herself thought of him only as the brother she had never had.

He was, however, her greatest friend, and because it was much more fun riding with him than with a groom, she invariably told him where they could meet.

Then they would race each other across the fields, or walk their horses in the woods and talk of all the things which interested Loretta, and which Christopher, because he loved her, attempted to understand.

When she rode up to him now he knew immediately that something was wrong.

"What has happened?" he asked.

She did not question that he knew instinctively that she was upset, but merely replied:

"I can hardly bear to tell you, Christopher, what Papa has arranged."

"What is it?"

"My . . marriage!"

Loretta said it dramatically, and there was silence. Then Christopher said in a strangled voice:

"Oh, my God! I knew this would happen sooner or later."

He was a good-looking young man of twenty-five years of age with broad shoulders and he rode the rather indifferent horse, which was all his father could afford, extremely well.

He had been in a good Regiment, but he had found it too expensive and had come home to try to manage the estate, and if possible, make it pay.

Because he loved Loretta overwhelmingly he had

recently been neglecting his duties quite considerably so that he could spend all the available time possible with her.

He knew his love was hopeless, he knew he had nothing to offer, and yet she filled his life completely.

He thought now that, even though her eyes were worried and her face was unmistakably pale, she looked very beautiful.

In fact, more beautiful then anyone he had ever seen in his whole life.

As Loretta told him what her father had said to her and what he had planned, Christopher Willoughby began to feel as if the whole world had gone dark.

Everything that mattered to him was lying shattered at his feet.

"You cannot become engaged to a man you have never even seen!" he said as Loretta paused for breath.

"That is what I told Papa, but he would not listen," she answered. "Christopher, what am I to do? I cannot marry a Frenchman with whom I have nothing in common, and live in France, far away from everything I have known and loved ever since I was a child!"

She was thinking as she spoke of the woods, the garden, and the countryside around her that had constituted her whole world until now.

"It is inhuman and it is wrong, absolutely wrong for you," Christopher said firmly.

"I knew you would understand," Loretta said, "but how can I make Papa see how cruelly he is treating me?"

There was no answer to this, and Christopher knew, as did everybody else in the neighbourhood, that once the Duke had made up his mind about something there was nothing anybody could do to change it.

"If Mama were alive," Loretta was saying, "I am sure she could have talked Papa into being more reasonable. After all, there is no reason why the *Marquis* should not come to England, and we could meet casually at a party or a Ball in London before there was any talk of our becoming engaged."

"And supposing you hated him?" Christopher suggested.

"Then I would have a chance to say 'no' when he asked me to marry him," Loretta replied. "As it is his father has already suggested we should be married and Papa has accepted on my behalf. All that is required now is for the *Marquis* to put the ring on my finger, and I am his wife!"

"You cannot do it!" Christopher exclaimed.

"But that is what will happen, unless I can, somehow, prevent it," Loretta said. "You know what Papa is like when he is in one of his obstinate moods, and he has always been impressed by the *Duc de* Sauerdun."

She paused a moment and then went on:

"I have heard so much about him and his horses over the years that I might almost own them."

"That is what you will do in time," Christopher said bitterly.

"I do not want them!" Loretta cried. "And I do not want his son either!"

Christopher drew in his breath.

"Will you run away with me, Loretta?"

Because she had been thinking only of herself, Loretta looked at him.

For the first time her eyes were no longer angry, but soft and gentle.

"Dear Christopher!" she said. "That is just the sort of thing you would suggest, and if I were in love with you, I would not hesitate."

"Then let me take you away," Christopher begged.

Loretta shook her head.

"Because I am so fond of you, I could not do anything which would spoil your life and eventually mine."

"Why, why?" Christopher asked. "I love you, Loretta, and I swear I would make you love me if you were my wife."

It was difficult for Loretta to tell him he was not in the least like her 'dream-man'.

He was kind, understanding, sympathetic and she was genuinely very fond of him.

But his offer was not what she wanted from life, not the love she had always envisaged and knew that when it came to her she would recognise it instantly.

She held out her hand and he took it as she said:

"Thank you, Christopher, for being so understanding, but the answer to my problem is not to run away with you, but to save myself in some other way from being married to a man I have never seen."

She paused a moment and then continued:

"For all I know, he may be abominable in every way, whatever Papa may say."

"It is not right that your father should make such a vital decision for you," Christopher said rather weakly.

He knew as he was speaking that it was in fact, quite a usual thing for somebody in the Duke's position to choose his daughter's future husband, without listening to anything she might say on the matter.

Although his father was relatively poor, he had been brought up in a society which believed that 'blue blood' should go to 'blue blood'.

Also where possible a man with a title should ensure that his marriage would bring either money or land into the family.

His father had never thought for one instant there was any chance of his marrying Loretta.

He had therefore continually dinned into his son's head that, if and when he married, he must choose a girl who had a large dowry.

"When you become the 6th Baronet, my boy," he

would say, "you and your son will not be in the plight we are now."

Christopher made one more desperate attempt on his own behalf to Loretta.

"Will you promise me," he said, "that if you really feel, when you meet him, that it is impossible for you to marry this man – and, God knows, I hate the thought of him – that you will tell me so, and let me take you away?"

"You mean elope?"

"We could be married by Special Licence," Christopher said. "Then at least even if you do not love me, it will not be so frightening or unpleasant for you as being married to a stranger."

"That is true," Loretta said slowly. "At the same time, Christopher, I intend to fight Papa and find some way of preventing him from announcing my engagement at the Ball he intends to give in Ascot week, when the Duke and his son are coming to stay with us."

"Why can he not come over before?" Christopher enquired. "It seems to me that he is behaving in an extra-ordinary manner. If you want to know at least what he looks like, one would expect him to feel the same."

"That is what I think," Loretta agreed, "but I suppose he is under his father's thumb and just has to do as he is told."

"Then he cannot be much of a man!" Christopher said firmly. "It seems to me a ridiculous situation that you are each sitting in your own country with the Channel be-tween you, and neither of you having the guts to meet each other."

He spoke violently, using a word which he would not ordinarily have used to Loretta, but she did not seem perturbed and only said:

"That has given me an idea, Christopher!"

"What has?"

"What you have just said. If the *Marquis* will not come to me, why should I not go to him?"

"How can you?" Christopher not unreasonably enquired. "The Duke had not invited you to stay, and as your father said, perhaps he has very good reasons for not doing so."

He realised as he spoke that he was being rather spiteful, but he was thinking that all was fair in love and war.

Loretta's huge eyes were fixed on his face as she said:

"You have been very clever! Far cleverer than I expected, Christopher!"

"I do not understand what you are saying."

"It is something I have to think out," Loretta said in a quiet voice.

Christopher was now rather alarmed.

"Now listen, Loretta, you are not to do anything outrageous! Whatever I said, the one thing you cannot do is to go to France. It would cause a frightful scandal if you did so without the *Duc de* Sauerdun giving you an invitation. What is more, you would then be committed to marrying his beastly son!"

"I am not so foolish as to do anything like that," Loretta said slowly.

"Then what are you thinking about? Tell me!" Christopher begged anxiously.

She laughed, then said:

"It is only an idea you have put into my head and thank you, Christopher. I feel better now that I have told you all about it, but I think I should now go home."

"No!" Christopher protested. "Let us ride together under the trees. You owe me that, Loretta, having given me news that will mean sleepless nights with the knowledge that sooner rather than later I will lose you."

Impulsively Loretta put out her hand again.

"You will never lose me completely, Christopher.

26

Whatever I do, or do not have to do, there will always be a place in my heart for you."

Her words brought a look of yearning to Christopher's eyes.

Then as Loretta took her hand away and rode her horse forward he followed her into the wood.

There were paths where there was just room for two horses to move together towards a clearing in the centre where the wood-cutters had been taking down a number of trees.

It was a place where they had often dismounted to sit and talk.

Because Loretta knew that Christopher was upset and in consequence might try to kiss her, she passed on through the clearing and deliberately rode to the other side of the wood.

They spoke very little. Christopher was content just to be beside her, even though he was suffering.

She knew that she had dealt him a body-blow when she told him she was to be married.

It had of course, always been inevitable, although she had not expected it to be so soon.

Christopher was very important in her life because he was her one confidant, the one companion whom she could trust, and to whom she could say anything that came into her head.

But she was not in love with him, and she knew that what she felt for him would never develop into love.

When finally at the end of the wood she said goodbye, she knew how unhappy he was, and she felt she had been cruel in telling him of her troubles.

But there was no one else to whom she could turn, and no one else she could trust.

"I will be waiting for you tomorrow afternoon, Loretta," Christopher said, "but if by any chance you want to see me before that, send Ben over with a note.

You can trust him not to talk."

"I expect Ben and everybody else knows that we see each other," Loretta said, "with the exception of course of Papa, and no one would dare tell him!"

"I hope not!"

Christopher had suggested meeting in the afternoon because he had so much work to do in the morning on the estate, and now he said again:

"Send Ben and I will come to you if you want me, as quickly as I can."

"Thank you, Christopher, and thank you for helping me. I do not feel as desperate as I did."

"Take care of yourself, Loretta."

She knew as he looked at her that the love in his eyes was very touching, but she told herself that however desperate she might feel, she could not imagine herself as Christopher's wife.

As she rode home alone she was pondering over what he had said and the thought in her mind was:

"If the *Marquis* will not come to see me, then I must go to see him."

But not as herself. That would surely be a mistake.

If she could only see him, find out what he was like as a man, how he behaved, then if, as she suspected, he was everything that was hateful, she would threaten her father that if he forced her to marry him, she would run away.

She had no idea where she would go, but at least she could make things very difficult if she just disappeared and they could not find her.

She was sure that if she did that and stayed away for some weeks or even months her father would capitulate.

Although he was difficult and shouted at her when he did not get things his own way, she knew now that her mother was dead that she was the most important person in his life and he really loved her.

'I have to see the *Marquis*,' she thought, 'but how can I do it?'

Suddenly, almost like the answer to a prayer, she remembered her Cousin Ingrid.

Loretta had always loved Ingrid who was six years older than she was and who had been married when she was seventeen, making what the Court families always said was a 'brilliant marriage'.

Her husband was a man thirty years older than she was, but the Earl of Wick was of great importance socially, and a very rich man.

Looking back, Loretta was certain that Ingrid had been given no choice in the matter of her marriage to the Earl.

She had been swept up the aisle by ambitious parents who were only too delighted that their daughter had, almost before leaving the School-Room, become of such social consequence.

Knowing nothing about men or love, Ingrid had found her husband dull and set in his ways.

He was anxious only that she should produce an heir to his title and be a competent hostess to his friends, who naturally were all, as he was, very much older than herself.

Year by year, as Ingrid matured she had become more and more beautiful.

It was obvious that she would eventually fall in love.

It was then that she met the Marquess of Galston out hunting.

Then the Earl of Wick took to leaving her alone in his large country house.

He went to shooting-parties, and attended Regimental dinners in London.

In the Autumn he preferred to stalk stags in Scotland at house-parties where he was undisturbed by women.

Ingrid was lonely, and because the Marquess of Galston was as disillusioned by marriage as she was, it was inevitable they should turn to each other for sympathy.

The Marquess had been married when he was young to a beautiful girl with whom he had thought himself very much in love, until he discovered how unstable and how hysterical she could be.

Within two years she was showing every sign of being mentally deranged.

Finally, although he fought against it, the doctors insisted that she should be put in a Private Nursing Home under the supervision of nurses who could cope with her case.

The Marquess and Ingrid poured out their troubles to each other and fell in love.

It was very different from anything the Marquess had ever felt before, or Ingrid had ever known.

Because they found life without each other intolerable, they had run away, causing a scandal that had re-verberated through the Marquess's family and that of the Duke.

Ingrid and the Marquess left England for France and never returned.

The Earl of Wick had divorced her after a long-drawn-out operation involving an Act of Parliament.

Unfortunately even when she was free it was impossible to marry the Marquess because his wife was still alive, although incurably insane.

Loretta remembered how in the family it had been forbidden to mention Ingrid again, though inevitably they sometimes talked of her in lowered voices and whispers.

If anybody came back from Paris where she and the Marquess were living, sooner or later, as if sheer curiosity overcome them, the Courts would ask in rather shocked voices:

"Did you, by any chance, see anything of Ingrid or the Marquess?"

Loretta could remember hearing this a dozen times, and because she had loved and admired her older cousin who had been very kind to her, she was always afraid that she would hear something unpleasant.

Perhaps the love she and the Marquess had had for each other had died and now they were parted?

However, there was no news except that Ingrid was looking exceedingly beautiful and had been seen at the Opera and other public places of amusement.

Of course no respectable people, Loretta was sure, such as the *Duc de* Sauerdun would know them.

They were 'living in sin', which barred them from being accepted by anyone who was aware of the disgraceful way in which they had both behaved.

Now almost as if it was a light in the darkness into which her father had plunged her, Loretta found herself thinking of Ingrid.

Ingrid would understand: Ingrid would know that it was impossible for her, Loretta, to be married, as she herself had been, to a man of whom she knew nothing.

A man she might hate and detest, or who might neglect her, as the Earl of Wick had neglected his wife.

As she saw through the trees her father's large, rather ugly mansion ahead of her, she thought there was something austere and even hard about it, which she had not noticed before.

Then she told herself triumphantly:

"I will see Ingrid and talk to her. If Papa will not understand what I am feeling – Ingrid will!"

# CHAPTER TWO

That evening at dinner the Duke informed Loretta that he was going to be away for a week.

"I shall be in Newmarket for the first four days," he said, "then I am going on for a couple of nights to your Cousin Marcus, who has a house in Suffolk."

"I believe he has some excellent horses, Papa," Loretta said.

"That is why I am going to stay with him," the Duke replied.

They talked on various other subjects, Loretta being careful not to refer again to the *Duc de* Sauerdun, and then after sitting quietly for a short time in the Drawing Room she went to bed early.

All that evening while talking to her father she had been planning in her mind an adventure that was so outrageous that she was almost afraid to contemplate it.

But she knew it was something she had to do, otherwise, whatever objections she might make, she would be married, and after that there would be no escape.

First thing the next morning, instead of riding in the woods as she usually did, Loretta went down to the village.

Living in one of her father's cottages was an old sewing-maid who had entered their service when her mother was alive.

She had only left after her death because she did not get on with the other servants.

Although Loretta was very fond of Marie, she knew she was a difficult woman who, because she was French, was rather like a 'fish out of water'.

She had come to England originally as lady's-maid to the French Ambassador's wife.

When at the end of her husband's term she had returned to Paris, Marie had stayed on.

Loretta had always thought she did so because she felt she had grown away from her own people and had no immediate family left, which was considered by the French to be essential.

She had therefore come to the Castle as sewing-maid, in which occupation she was extremely skilful.

Because she really was difficult and the other servants disliked her, she had accepted a cottage in the village.

Loretta often took clothes to her knowing Marie sewed much better than any English seamstress could have done because she had been taught in a French Convent.

As Loretta dismounted outside the pretty little cottage at the end of the village and tethered her horse to the railings, she wondered if Marie would welcome what she intended to ask her, or if she would refuse.

She knocked on the door and almost immediately it was opened by Marie, looking, Loretta thought, younger than her fifty-five years.

Despite the fact that she was not expecting visitors, she was dressed neatly and with what could only be described as an elegance which was essentially French.

"*Milady!*" she exclaimed when she saw Loretta. "*Quelle surprise.*"

"I have come to see you on a very important matter," Loretta said, as she walked into the small cottage.

As she expected, it was spotlessly clean.

Marie, like all good French housewives, hung her

bedding out of her windows every day to get the air, and considered the English very slovenly because they did not do the same.

"You would like coffee, *Milady*?" Marie asked.

"I would love some!" Loretta replied.

She knew if anything could break the ice when she talked to Marie it would be if they were sharing a pot of the excellent coffee on which Marie spent a good portion of her pension.

While Marie busied herself preparing the coffee, and poured it into cups which were polished as if they were glass, Loretta considered what she should say.

Then she decided the best thing to do was to tell Marie the truth.

Accordingly as they drank the coffee she told Marie of the Duke's intention to marry her off to the *Marquis de* Sauerdun, and saw the old maid's eyes light up with excitement.

"*Le Duc de* Sauerdun a verry great aristocrat!" she murmured.

"I know that," Loretta said. "At the same time, Marie, although being French you will not understand, I refuse to be pushed into marriage with a man I have never seen, whom I may hate as soon as I meet him, and who may hate me!"

Marie did not speak and Loretta went on:

"I have therefore decided to go to France to visit my Cousin Ingrid, who is living in Paris. I am sure she will arrange that I will somehow meet the *Duc* without his being aware of who I am."

Marie stared at her in astonishment. At the same time, her quick brain was assimilating exactly what Loretta intended.

"*C'est impossible, Milady!*" she said firmly. "Countess of Wick no longer accepted by *votre Père*."

"I know that, Marie," Loretta agreed, "but as she is

34

the only person I know who lives in Paris, I must go to her and tell her what I want to do. Therefore, unless you wish me to go alone, which I would find rather frightening, we are leaving, you and I, tomorrow."

Marie stared at her as if she thought she had taken leave of her senses. Then she repeated:

"Tomorrow? *Non, non! Ma petite*, that is something you cannot do!"

"It is something I have every intention of doing!" Loretta replied. "I shall be upset, Marie, if you will not come with me, but I shall have to go alone. There is no-one, as you well know, up at the house whom I can trust not to tell Papa what I am doing."

"That is true," Marie agreed. "Those stupid servants run at once to tell *Milord*, and he would be verry angry."

"Very angry indeed!" Loretta added. "And you know, Marie, it is no use trying to talk to him about it or trying to make him see my point of view. He has made up his mind, and that is that!"

Marie made a gesture that was typically French, which told Loretta that what she was saying was indisputable.

She had spent long enough at the Castle to know exactly how dictatorial the Duke could be when it suited him.

His rages were feared by everybody from the Butler down to the lowliest scullion of the kitchen.

"Now, what we are going to do," Loretta said, "is to set off for France the very moment Papa has left for Newmarket. He will go early because he will drive first to the station to take a train to London, which will enable him to have luncheon at his Club before he travels on to Newmarket."

Marie nodded and Loretta went on:

"We will drive across country, and catch a train that will take us to Dover in time to catch the afternoon Steamer to Calais."

Marie threw up her hands.

"You everything planned, *Milady*! But have you thought what fuss there'll be when they discover you are gone?"

"There is no reason why anybody should know where I have gone," Loretta said. "I shall tell them at the house that I am going to stay with friends since Cousin Emily is still confined to her bed."

She paused a moment and then added:

"Emily will be only too glad to be rid of me and have nothing to do until Papa returns."

Marie looked a little fearful and Loretta put out her hand and laid it on hers.

"Please help me," she pleaded. "You know that I should not go to France without you, for you will know exactly how to get me to Paris, and how I can find Cousin Ingrid once I get there."

Marie rose as Loretta spoke and went to a drawer.

She opened it and brought out a bundle of what Loretta saw were pieces out of the newspapers.

As she looked at them she saw that all the top ones referred to the race-meetings in France where her father's horses had won.

Beneath these were several cuttings about the Marquess of Galston and the Countess of Wick.

"Where did you get these, Marie?" she asked.

"I have in France an old friend I not see for twenty years, but he writes to me and since he verry interested in horses I send him reports of His Grace's when they win big races an' he send me pieces from the French *journeaux*."

Loretta turned them over quickly.

There were four or five that referred to the English beauty, the Countess of Wick.

One, more recent than the others, reported that the Marquess of Galston had bought a house in the Avenue des Champs-Élysées.

It described the decoration and the contents of the house and finished by saying:

*"The hostess at the Marquess's parties will be the beautiful English Countess of Wick."*

As Loretta read it she realised how shocked her relations would be at a newspaper referring so blatantly to the relationship between the Marquess and Ingrid.

But that did not concern her at the moment.

What was important was that she now knew where to go when she reached Paris.

The cuttings went back over several years and having looked at those that referred to her father's horses she said:

"Thank you, Marie. I knew you would help me. Will you be ready at eight-thirty tomorrow morning, when I will pick you up?"

Marie did not hesitate, but said with a smile:

"I come with you, *Milady,* an' it'll make me verry happy see *la belle France* again."

"Of course it will," Loretta agreed, "and with any luck we will be back before Papa returns from his visit and he will never have the slightest idea what I have been doing in his absence."

She thought as she spoke she ought to keep her fingers crossed.

At the same time, she was well aware that it was lucky that she had Marie to turn to.

Any of the servants in the house would have been far too frightened to go with her knowing that if the Duke discovered it he would certainly dismiss them for doing so.

"Eight-thirty, Marie," Loretta said again, "and thank you for the coffee!"

As she went from the cottage she knew that Marie

would be excitedly packing what she would require for the journey.

As she had said, it would be very thrilling for her to return to he own country after being away for so long.

When Loretta arrived home she sent for the maid who looked after her and told her to pack what she required.

"You are going away, M'Lady?"

"Yes, I am going to stay with friends. But I have not yet told His Grace, so please do not mention it to anyone. You know it will only worry him when he is concerned with everything else that has to be done in his absence. I am only telling you, Sarah, that I am going, so do not say anything to the rest of the staff."

She knew that Sarah, who was very fond of her, would do as she asked.

At the same time, she was hoping her father would not be too inquisitive as to how she would occupy her time in her absence.

Fortunately the Duke was busily concerned with his own affairs.

He assumed that as Loretta had not referred again to her wedding to the *Marquis* she had accepted it, and he was in an exceedingly good humour.

"Look after yourself while I am away," he said, "and I hope that your cousin will soon be better, otherwise you may find it rather lonely without me."

"I shall miss you terribly, Papa, as I always do," Loretta replied. "But I shall be quite happy looking after the horses, so do not worry about me, and as soon as Cousin Emily is better, perhaps we shall be able to go shopping."

The Duke was just about to ask his daughter for what purpose, when he realised what she was referring to.

He smiled to himself.

No woman, he thought, could resist the allurement of a trousseau.

He was quite certain that any rebellious feelings Loretta

might have would soon be forgotten when she was buying new clothes and above all, planning her wedding-gown.

He drove off the next morning in a flurry in case he missed the train.

Papers were forgotten at the last moment, and every servant in the house seemed to be running up and down the stairs for something or other he required.

When at last he was gone it was not yet eight o'clock and Loretta realised she had all the time she wanted.

She ordered a carriage drawn by the fastest horses that had not already left with her father, and then went to find his passport.

It was in the drawer of a table where he always kept it and consisted of a large single sheet of heavily engraved paper signed by the Foreign Secretary.

It was a passport the Duke had used for many years and he often boasted of the number of times he had crossed the Channel.

It still had her mother's name on it, and as it was hand-written in copper-plate writing, it was not difficult for Loretta to add her own name so skilfully that it would have taken a very observant official to suspect that it had not been done in the Post Office.

Then she remembered she had not asked Marie if she had a passport.

She felt certain, however, that though it was long ago that the maid had come to England, she would never have discarded anything so precious as a passport.

It would entitle her to return to her own country if ever she wished to do so.

Loretta found her assumption was correct.

On arriving outside Marie's cottage she saw the Frenchwoman waiting just inside the doorway with a small piece of baggage beside her.

In a low voice so that no-one could overhear Loretta asked:

"You have your passport, Marie?"

"*Oui, Milady!* I would not lose anythin' so precious."

Marie got into the carriage after she had carefully locked the door of her cottage and put the key in her handbag.

Loretta thought, she was looking exactly as a maid should, wearing a black cape which looked warm and practical, with a black bonnet, the ribbons tied under her chin.

The only touch of colour was a blue scarf around her neck which peeped out from under the collar of her cape.

Her grey hair was neatly arranged and her eyes were shining with excitement.

Loretta thought once again how fortunate it had been that Marie was available to travel with her to look after her.

They caught a train which took them to a junction on the main line to Dover, and were fortunate that they had only twenty-five minutes to wait before the train from London arrived.

This carried them to the coast in time, as Loretta had anticipated, to catch the afternoon Steamer across the Channel.

Something Loretta had not forgotten was that she would need plenty of money, and she had quite shamelessly pilfered the stock of cash which her father always kept in a special locked drawer of his desk.

The Duke's secretary paid the servants their wages, but, because her father never trusted anyone except himself, the money was kept in his desk until it was required.

There was a considerable sum there, and Loretta took rather more than she thought she would require.

At the same time, she was not so greedy as to leave the stock much depleted, which she was sure would upset the secretary.

He was a nervous, elderly man, who always looked

as if he carried all the cares of the world upon his shoulders.

To make sure there was no trouble, she said to the Butler before she left:

"Will you tell Mr. Miller when he comes in that His Grace gave me some money for my visit out of his special drawer, and I will repay it when I get back."

"Very good, M'Lady," the Butler replied.

"I only hope I have thought of everything!" Loretta had wondered as she drove down the drive.

When the Steamer that was waiting for them at Dover began to leave the harbour she told herself with an irrepressible excitement that she had won!

She had got away without any fuss, and now she should be able to see the *Marquis* and form some opinion about him, and to return home without anyone being aware that she had been to France.

Being well able to afford it, she had taken a cabin on the Steamer, and to keep Marie happy had ordered the steward to bring them coffee and biscuits immediately.

"I thought we had better wait to eat on the train," Loretta said. "I am rather afraid if the sea is rough that I will be sea-sick."

"I not afraid of *mal de mer, Milady*. When I come here from France many years ago, ship not big, an' passengers verry sick. But I all right. I verry good sailor. Everyone say so."

"I hope I am as good as you," Loretta replied, "but I have never been to sea before."

She thought as she spoke that, if she married the *Marquis*, it would be something she would do continually, if she wished to visit England as often as his father did.

It seemed strange that he had always stayed in France while his father the *Duc* seldom missed an important race-meeting in England.

In just the same way her father constantly attended meetings at Chantilly and Longchamps.

They reached Calais in two hours because the wind was with them, and the train to Paris was waiting at the quay-side.

Loretta left it to Marie to get them the best accommodation that was available.

She managed to get a reserved carriage.

As the Calais-Paris was one of the corridor trains, which had been introduced nine years earlier, there were stewards only too anxious to wait on them and bring them everything they wanted.

After they had enjoyed an excellent meal, which was really a kind of light and early dinner, Loretta, who had hardly slept the night before, went over her plans.

She was worrying in case something would prevent her from leaving at the last minute.

Then she fell asleep.

When she awoke, it was to find that it was dark outside and they were due in Paris in half-an-hour.

"You not tell me, *Milady*," Marie said, "where we go when in Paris, to zee house of the Marquess, or first to an Hotel."

It was something Loretta had not really considered until now, but finally after a little thought she said:

"I think we will try first the Marquess's house. If everybody has gone to bed we will go away until the morning."

Marie laughed.

"In Paris no one go bed early!"

That was what Marie thought, Loretta smiled to herself, but she had not been in France for many years and perhaps things had changed since then.

Or perhaps the Marquess and Ingrid, being social outcasts, were living very quietly and unable to entertain in the ordinary way.

When they reached the *Gard du Nord* it was nearly midnight.

A porter found them a *fiacre* and they set off towards the Champs-Élysées.

"If the house looks dark and there are no lights in the windows," Loretta said, speaking more to herself than to Marie, "we will turn around and go to the Hotel Meurice. I know that is where Papa stays when he comes to Paris."

Marie said nothing, but Loretta knew she was thinking it was very improper for an unmarried girl, even with a lady's-maid, to stay in an Hotel.

The *fiacre* reached the Avenue des Champs-Élysées and drew up outside a house with its front enclosed by iron railings tipped with gold.

Loretta saw there was a large number of private carriages with liveried attendants waiting outside.

There were linkmen with torches shining for those who were wanted by their employers.

She was certain that the coachman had brought them to the wrong house by mistake.

"You are sure this is the house we require?" she asked in her excellent Parisian French. "The mansion of the Marquess of Galston?"

"*Oui, oui, Madame, c'est vrai!*" the coachman insisted.

"You wait, *Milady*," Marie said. "I find out."

She got out of the *fiacre* as she spoke, and walking up to the front door spoke to a servant wearing an impressive gold-braided livery.

The man and Marie gesticulated briefly to each other, for, as Loretta remembered, the French seemed unable to speak without using their hands.

Then Marie returned all smiles.

"This right, *Milady*, ze home of *Monsieur le Marquess*, an' he has party."

Loretta suddenly felt shy.

43

"Perhaps . . .?" she began.

Then the servant who had followed Marie opened the door and somehow she felt compelled to step out.

"Perhaps we had better ask the coachman to wait, Marie," she began again in French, "in case we are not welcome."

But it was too late.

Marie had already given orders for the luggage to be taken down and was paying with the francs which they had obtained aboard the Steamer at what Loretta guessed was a very poor rate of exchange.

There was nothing she could do therefore but follow the servant into the house, aware that the Hall looked very grand, decorated with huge vases of exotic flowers.

Several guests were coming down the stairs from what was obviously a Reception Room on the first floor, all men and they were laughing and talking as they did so.

Then as Loretta reached the top of the stairs a servant asked:

"What name shall I say, *Madame*?"

As he spoke, over his shoulder Loretta saw Ingrid standing near the doorway, looking exceedingly lovely and glittering with jewels in her hair, around her neck and in her ears.

For a moment Loretta just stood looking at her, while the servant waited for her name.

Then Ingrid turned and saw her, and there was no doubt of the astonishment in her eyes as Loretta ran towards her.

"Ingrid, you remember me?" she asked a little breathlessly.

"Loretta! Whatever are you doing here?"

"I have come to see you. I had to see you!"

Ingrid looked bewildered and Loretta said:

"Papa does not know I have left England, but I had to come because there was no one else to help me!"

As if she was too bemused to think clearly, Ingrid kissed Loretta and said:

"But, of course, dearest, I will do anything I can. Where are you staying?"

"With you if you will have me."

Again Ingrid stared at Loretta as if she could not have heard properly what she had said. Then she said quickly:

"We must talk about it. My guests are just leaving, let me say good-bye to them first."

"Of course," Loretta agreed. "I do apologise for bursting in on you like this."

As she spoke Ingrid stepped in front of her to shake hands with a man who was obviously waiting for her to attend to him.

"*Au revoir, Monsieur!*" she said.

"*Au revoir*, lovely lady," the gentleman replied in French. "Needless to say, I have never enjoyed an evening more or been more stimulated by the conversation. I hope you will invite me again soon."

"But of course," Ingrid replied. "How can we have a party without you?"

The Frenchman kissed her hand, then as he moved away another gentleman took his place and almost the same conversation was repeated.

It was only as the last guest left the room and the Marquess escorted him to the top of the stairs, that Loretta realised there were no ladies present at the party.

The guests were exclusively men, some of whom seemed elderly, but all of them had a distinguished appearance.

Ingrid turned to where she was standing behind her and said:

"Now Loretta dearest, do tell me what all this is about! I cannot imagine what you are doing here, and, as you say, alone."

"I have Marie with me. You remember Marie who used to sew for us at the Castle?"

"Yes, of course I remember Marie. Does nobody else know that you have come to me?"

"No one," Loretta replied with a smile. "Papa has gone away to Newmarket races for a week and has not the slightest idea that I intended coming to France."

As she finished speaking the Marquess came towards them and Ingrid said:

"Hugh, darling, what am I to do? This is my cousin, Loretta Court, who has just arrived in Paris to see me, because she says she needs my help."

"Then of course you must try to help her," the Marquess replied.

He was an exceedingly attractive man and Loretta could understand immediately why Ingrid had fallen in love with him.

He put out his hand and said:

"How do you do, Lady Loretta! And welcome, even though your visit was not anticipated!"

Loretta looked up at him and pleaded:

"Please, let me stay with you for a few days. I am in trouble, terrible trouble, and the only person I knew would understand and help me was Ingrid!"

"Then of course you must be my guest," the Marquis said.

He looked at Ingrid as he spoke and she said in a low voice:

"Are we wise to let her stay? After all . . ."

"No one need know that I am here," Loretta said quickly, "and it would be best for reasons I will explain to you, Ingrid, if I could stay under another name. I have warned Marie not to say who I am until I have explained to you why I have come."

"That certainly would make things easier," Ingrid said in a low voice, "at the same time, I am sure . . ."

"Stop worrying," the Marquis said. "I know exactly what you are thinking, my darling, but all that matters is that it is very late, your cousin has been travelling all day, and I think we should offer her something to eat and drink before we trouble ourselves about anything else."

"Of course, Hugh, you are always so sensible," Ingrid said, "and I will do as you say."

She spoke in a caressing voice, and the look in her eyes told Loretta that she was still very much in love with the man with whom she had run away.

Then Ingrid slipped her arm through Loretta's and said:

"Let us go to sit somewhere more cosy and Hugh will bring you a glass of champagne."

"First I will arrange for your cousin's luggage to be brought in and taken up to her room," the Marquess said, "then make sure her maid is looked after."

"I am certain Marie is making herself at home," Loretta said to Ingrid. "She was very excited at the idea of coming to France, and I knew there was no one else I could trust not to run to tell Papa."

"I can still hardly believe that you are here," Ingrid said. "But you know, dearest, much as I love you, it is wrong for you to associate with me."

"Nonsense!" Loretta said. "As long as you are happy, I am sure you did the right thing. But because you did run away, that is why I have come to you for advice."

"You are not saying .. you are much too young to be ..." Ingrid began, a little incoherently and Loretta said quickly:

"No, I am not running away *with* anyone! I am only running *from* the man whom Papa has chosen for me as a husband."

By this time Ingrid had opened the door of a very attractive and comfortable-looking Sitting-Room.

Because it looked so cosy and so lived in, Loretta was certain it was where she and the Marquess sat when they were alone.

As soon as they were inside, Ingrid, without saying any more, helped Loretta to take off the cloak she had worn for travelling and the small bonnet she had worn on her fair hair.

"Sit down, dearest," she said. "I can still hardly believe first that you really are here, and secondly that you are old enough to be married."

"Of course I am!" Loretta said. "I am over eighteen, and it is only because I was in mourning for Mama that I was not presented last year."

"But you are to be presented this year?"

"I am to be deprived of all the excitements of the Season I was promised simply because Papa wishes to announce my engagement in Ascot week and has already arranged for my marriage to take place almost immediately afterwards."

"But why? Why the hurry?" Ingrid enquired.

"That is what I am determined to find out!" Loretta said. "And that is why I have come to you."

"I am very flattered you have done so, although from your point of view it could do you harm. But I do not at all understand how I can help you."

Loretta paused for a moment. Then she said:

"The husband whom Papa has chosen for me is the son of a man he meets racing and with whom he is very impressed."

She looked at her cousin as she said slowly:

"He is a Frenchman, the *Duc de* Sauerdun!"

There was a silence, which to Loretta seemed very significant. Then Ingrid said with an incredulous note in her voice:

"Are you saying that your father wants you to marry

Fabian, the *Marquis de* Sauerdun?"

"That is right," Loretta said, "and he is determined that I shall do so."

"But, no! That is impossible!" Ingrid exclaimed "Completely and utterly impossible! Anyone, almost anyone but not Fabian!"

Her voice seemed to ring out. Then as Loretta stared at her she said in a different tone:

"I know I should not speak to you like that, but you are so young, and so beautiful! Because I have always loved you, Loretta, I would never wish you to make an unhappy marriage, as I did."

"That is why I came to you," Loretta said simply, "for I knew you would understand. Papa simply would not listen to me when I said I must get to know him before he comes to England. Otherwise as soon as he comes whatever I may feel I know we shall be formally engaged."

"It is intolerable," Ingrid exclaimed, "quite intolerable that Cousin Arthur, a man I have always admired, should treat you like this!"

"You know what Papa is like when he makes up his mind," Loretta said, "and he has always had a great admiration for the *Duc de* Sauerdun because he owns such fine race-horses."

"Race-horses are one thing – marriage is another!"

"You tell that to Papa! He will not listen to me!"

"He is certainly not likely to listen to me," Ingrid said with a little grimace.

Because there was a note of bitterness in Ingrid's voice, Loretta suddenly remembered her situation and she said:

"I have longed and longed to know if you were happy and if it was worth while running away as you did."

"It was the most sensible thing I have ever done in my whole life!" Ingrid replied. "I thank God every day of my life for the happiness I have with Hugh. At the same time, my lovely little cousin, this is not the life for you at your age."

Loretta looked puzzled and Ingrid explained:

"You would be married to Fabian de Sauerdun, which of course is different. At the same time, he would be impossible as a husband, completely and absolutely impossible!"

Loretta gave a little gasp but did not speak, and Ingrid went on:

"So sooner or later, I would always be sure that you would have to do what I did, run away with someone who would understand you and would be as kind, gentle and marvellous as Hugh has been to me."

Loretta gave a little sigh.

"That is the sort of . . love I . . want."

"Of course you do. It is what we all want," Ingrid agreed.

"And you are convinced that I would not find it with the *Marquis*?"

"I should say it was impossible for any woman to be happy with him for long," Ingrid answered.

"But why?"

"It is difficult to put into words, but you would understand if you saw him."

"That is exactly what I have come here to do!"

Ingrid looked at Loretta in surprise and she explained:

"I want you to arrange for me to meet the *Marquis* without his knowing who I am. I want to see him simply as a man, not as a husband already arranged for me."

She drew in her breath.

"I want to be able to explain to Papa exactly why I will not marry him, however much he may rage at me and even punish me for refusing to do so!"

"Now I understand why you have come," Ingrid said, "but it will be difficult, very difficult for you to meet the

50

*Marquis* and have him pay any attention to you, so that you can get to know exactly what he is like."

"I do not understand," Loretta said.

Ingrid smiled, and it made her look very lovely.

"Fabian de Sauerdun is the most sought after, the most fêted and acclaimed man in the whole of Paris! Every woman runs after him! They fall into his arms before he even has time to ask their names!"

Loretta looked astonished and Ingrid went on:

"When he leaves them, as is inevitable because he is quickly bored, they break their hearts, they threaten suicide!"

"Suicide!" Loretta exclaimed.

"It has become an accepted joke in Paris," Ingrid continued, "that he is a modern 'Casanova', a breaker of hearts who is never faithful to any woman for more than a few months."

As Ingrid finished speaking she gave what was almost a little sob as she said:

"Poor little Loretta! How can you possibly cope with a man like that?"

"Of course I could not," Loretta replied, "and that is exactly what I have come to find out. Unfortunately the person I have to convince is Papa, and I doubt if he will listen to me."

She thought as she spoke that her only alternative was to run away with Christopher.

She had only seen Ingrid and the Marquess together for a few minutes.

But she knew what they felt for each other was something she would never in a million years feel for Christopher Willoughby.

"I do not know what I can do about you," Ingrid said in a low voice.

"I have to see the *Marquis* for myself . . that is essential!" Loretta said. "What I am asking you to do, Ingrid,

51

is to dress me up, and give me a new name!"

She paused a moment and then went on:

"Let me meet him as a friend of yours, but certainly not as the daughter of the Duke of Madrescourt."

Ingrid looked at her before she said:

"I suppose your father and Fabian's are behind all this."

"Yes, of course," Loretta agreed. "I am sure the *Marquis* has no more wish to marry me than I have to marry him, but our respective fathers have concocted it between them on the race-course."

She wrinkled her forehead as she said:

"The only thing I do not understand is why the *Duc* should be in such a hurry about it."

"I can answer that question," Ingrid said. "The *Duc* is, I am sure, worried because Fabian has become involved with an extremely attractive and exotic type of woman whom it would be just possible for him to marry."

"What do you mean by that?" Loretta asked.

"If she were a *demi-mondaine*, then there would be no question of marriage, but the woman in question, while by no means the equal of the Sauerduns by birth or blood, is what one can call a Lady."

Ingrid gave a little laugh before she added:

"She was also married for a short time to a man who was undoubtedly a gentleman. I am putting it into English words, but in French it would sound very different."

"What is a '*demi-mondaine*'?" Loretta asked.

For a moment Ingrid stared at her, then she said after a pause:

"It is a name for a woman of a different social standing."

"So that is the reason why the *Duc* is determined his son shall make a good marriage."

"Of course," Ingrid said, "and who better than yourself?"

Loretta got to her feet.

"I will not do it! I have to convince Papa it is impossible! But first I must convince myself. Please, Ingrid, let me meet him! Let me see exactly what he is like. Then perhaps I shall be eloquent enough on the subject to make Papa see that there are other men in the world besides the *Duc de* Sauerdun's son."

Ingrid gave a deep sigh.

"It is going to be difficult, very, very difficult, Loretta! But to save you from making a mess of your life, as I originally made of mine, I will do anything, anything, dearest, that you ask of me!"

# CHAPTER THREE

"One thing you must realise," Ingrid said, "is that Fabian will take no notice of you if he thinks you are a *jeune fille*."

Loretta looked surprised and her cousin explained:

"It is the policy of all sophisticated men to ignore young girls, largely because they are afraid of being pressurised into marriage if they so much as talk to one."

She laughed before she went on:

"You can therefore imagine that the more sophisticated beauties, to whichever side of the Channel they belong, encourage this idea, and I am sure Fabian has never talked to a *jeune fille* unless she was a relation."

"Then if I am to talk to him as I want to, what am I to do?" Loretta asked a little helplessly.

She was lying back against the pillows of an exceedingly comfortable bed.

It was draped with curtains and the room in which she was sleeping was very palatial, with fine Louis XIV furniture, which she much appreciated.

Marie, who chattered away like a parakeet because she was so thrilled to be back in her beloved France, had brought her breakfast at her usual time of eight o'clock.

With it came instructions that she was to stay in bed

54

until the Countess came to see her.

"Very nice house, M'Lady," Marie said appreciatively, "everyone verry 'appy, *c'est toujours même chose en France!*"

She spoke almost defiantly.

Loretta had to prevent herself from laughing knowing that Marie would point out in no uncertain terms how difficult the English were compared to her own countrymen.

She drank the fragrant coffee that seemed much more delicious than what was provided at home and also the *croissants*, hot from the oven.

They were so light that she thought they might float away!

Then Ingrid came into her bedroom.

She was wearing a *négligée* and was, Loretta thought so lovely and attractive that she could understand why the Marquess looked at her with adoration in his eyes.

"Did you sleep well, dearest," Ingrid asked as she sat down on the side of the bed.

"Like a top!" Loretta answered. "I was not only tired, I was so thankful and relieved to have reached you, no longer to be as worried as I have been every night since Papa told me who I was to marry."

"I am afraid there is still a great deal to worry about," Ingrid said, "and I have been awake in the night because, my dearest little cousin, you have brought me one of the most difficult problems I have ever faced in my whole life."

She paused, then with an impish smile she added:

"Except of course, when I was trying to make up my mind whether or not to run away with Hugh!"

"Was that very difficult?"

"It was difficult because I loved him so much that I did not want to hurt him," Ingrid replied, "and I am still always afraid he will regret having to abandon his an-

55

cestral home with its great estate, and so many of his friends."

"I thought the moment I saw him how happy he looked," Loretta said.

Ingrid clasped her hands together.

"That is what I try to make him, and I pray that one day, if God is merciful, we will be able to be married, and have the children both of us want so desperately."

Loretta knew what Ingrid was saying.

It was that if the Marquess's wife died, then all would be plain-sailing as far as they were concerned.

At the same time, she could not help asking:

"When you are married, will you be able to come back to England?"

"I often ask myself that question," Ingrid replied in a low voice, "and I think the answer is a rather uncomfortable one."

She sighed and then went on:

"Although I will marry Hugh the moment his wife dies, I think it will still be difficult for us to return to England for perhaps many years."

There was a painful note in her voice which Loretta did not miss.

She understood that as long as the Earl of Wick was alive it would be embarrassing for him if his divorced wife was in the same country.

Perhaps too it would make people more unkind to Ingrid than they would be otherwise.

She knew it was unlikely that most of the Court family would ever forgive her. Yet, as her Nanny used to say, 'Time heals everything!'.

The older generation might continue to disapprove and be determined to punish Ingrid for her sins.

But the younger members of the family would accept her as the Marchioness of Galston if only because her husband was rich and important.

Impulsively Loretta bent forward and put her hands over Ingrid's as she said:

"I shall pray very, very hard, Ingrid dearest, that one day you will be as happy as you deserve to be."

"I am happy now!" Ingrid said defiantly. "At the same time I do not want you to make a mistake. The greatest one I ever made was to be married when I was seventeen to a man who was thirty years older than I was."

"I cannot accuse Papa of making me do that," Loretta smiled.

"That is true, but your position would be very much the same as mine," Ingrid said.

"Why?" Loretta enquired.

"Because most Frenchmen, and Fabian would be no exception, leave their wives in the country producing babies while they enjoy themselves in Paris with the glamorous women who have earned for the Capital of France the envy, or the disapproval, whichever way you look at it, of all Europe."

Loretta laughed.

"I know what our relations think of Paris, especially as you are living here."

"You need not tell me," Ingrid said, "I can guess exactly what they say! But where Fabian is concerned, it is not only the attractions of Paris that will worry me."

She sighed before adding:

"It is that you, my dearest, will break your heart over him as so many other women have done."

"I understand exactly what you have been saying to me," Loretta answered. "That is why I am determined if as you say he is a modern Casanova, that Papa shall not make me marry him."

Her voice deepened as she added:

"It would be bound to make me desperately unhappy until I found somebody like your charming Marquess."

Ingrid gave a little cry of horror.

57

"How can you possibly envisage doing that before you are even married?" she asked. "I have been lucky, very lucky, because Hugh is different from most Englishmen. Because miraculously he loves me with his whole heart and soul, he really does not hanker after everything that was familiar and important to him before he met me."

Her voice softened as she went on:

"I know only too well that any other English gentleman would be longing to shoot in the Autumn, to hunt in the Winter, and would perhaps miss more than anything else his Clubs at which he could always find men with whom he had been at School or University."

She paused for a moment before she said:

"If Hugh has ever been homesick for any of those things, he has never let me be aware of it. But you can understand that I am always on edge, always waiting for the moment when he first regrets that he has done anything so socially outrageous as to run away with – another man's wife."

Because the way in which Ingrid was speaking was so moving, Loretta could only put out her arms and kiss her before she said:

"I love you for being so frank with me, and I understand what you are saying. So, unless I am to find myself in the position you were in, you have to help me."

Ingrid put her hands up to her forehead as she said:

"I have been thinking and thinking how to do that, and although it seems outrageous, Hugh and I have decided that the best thing we can do is to let you meet Fabian in a somewhat reprehensible manner."

"What do you mean by that?" Loretta asked a little nervously.

"He is in fact, coming here today for luncheon."

"Today?" Loretta cried.

"Yes," Ingrid said. "Hugh wanted to put him off, but I

58

thought there was no point in trying to hide you away while we talked about it. Gossip flies on the wind in Paris, and unless we are careful everybody will know we have a young and very beautiful girl staying here."

"Then what can I do?" Loretta asked anxiously.

As she spoke she had visions of Ingrid sending her away to an Hotel or somewhere else where she would be alone and the idea was frightening.

"What we have to do," Ingrid said slowly, "is to transform you from a *jeune fille* into a woman of about the same age as myself, and who is married."

Loretta looked at her wide-eyed as she said:

"You look very young, but if you are dressed in a more sophisticated manner, and if your face is slightly made-up as is acceptable in Paris, I doubt if Fabian will suspect that you are not what we tell him you are."

Ingrid gave a little laugh as she said:

"One thing is absolutely certain – he will not expect to find a pure and innocent English débutante staying in the same house as the notorious Countess of Wick!"

"If I am supposed to be married," Loretta said, "what shall I say about my husband?"

"As little as possible!" Ingrid replied. "Obviously being an Englishman, he is inattentive and stupid, preferring sport to being with his wife. Otherwise of course, he would not have allowed you to come to Paris. In fact, we might insinuate, although not too obviously, that your husband has other *interests* besides yourself."

"What do you mean .. other interests?" Loretta enquired.

Ingrid realised that in her innocence she had no idea what this implied and she therefore said quickly:

"Sport being one, horses another, and of course he could be somewhat – enamoured of an attractive actress."

"Oh .. I see what you mean!" Loretta said. "Yes, of

59

course, that is an excellent idea, and it explains why I am on my own."

"Exactly! And now, dearest, you must get up and we will start the transformation for the part you have to play."

She stood up as she spoke and Loretta jumped out of bed and walked across the room to look out of the window.

"I am so excited at being in Paris," she said, "and *Marquis* or no *Marquis* I must see a little of what I know is the most thrilling Capital in the whole world."

"It is very beautiful at this time of the year when the chestnut trees are in bloom," Ingrid said, "and of course you must see Paris, dearest. I want you to remember your first visit as enjoyable, in spite of your worries over the naughty *Marquis*."

Then as if she thought they had talked enough, Ingrid became extremely efficient, and directed Loretta as if she thought she was on the stage.

'This is appropriate,' she told herself, 'because after all, if I am to be convincing, I have to be a good actress.'

While Loretta bathed, Ingrid went back to her own room and dressed.

When she came back she brought with her her lady's-maid who carried a pile of gowns over her arm.

"To begin with," she said, "because we have no time to shop, I am going to lend you my clothes. But if you are to see Fabian again, you must buy some new and exciting models which, as Paris is always so advanced in fashion, you can wear when you return home, if not this year, then definitely next."

It flashed through Loretta's mind that what she was buying might have to be part of her trousseau.

Then she thrust the thought away and concentrated on doing exactly what her cousin told her.

First Ingrid insisted on her wearing a small black lace corset of a kind she had never seen before.

"Your figure is perfect," she said, "but we have to make it fashionable with the smallest possible waist, and that means, whether you like it or not, tight lacing!"

Actually, Loretta found it not uncomfortable, but merely a little restricting.

The tightness of her corset made her feel she must hold herself very upright.

Then Ingrid made her try on gown after gown until she found one that she thought more suitable than any of the others.

It was the blue of Loretta's eyes, and was sensational, as only the French could design a gown without making it too flamboyant.

It had little touches of darker blue on it which gave it *chic*, and made it different from anything Loretta had ever worn before.

It certainly made her appear very much more sophisticated than her own gowns did.

When they had decided what she should wear, Ingrid's lady's-maid started to arrange her hair in a typically French style.

She piled it high on top of her head and so skilfully that Marie, who was watching, kept exclaiming:

"*C'est merveilleux! Milady* looks verry different from *les jeunes filles Anglaises*."

Loretta knew that Marie was referring to the pictures she had seen in '*The Ladies Journal*' which she bought so that she could try to copy the gowns they illustrated.

She knew Marie was right.

Both her hair and her gown were now essentially French, and they made her not only look different, but also feel different.

Ingrid had still not finished.

She herself applied a small amount of powder to

Loretta's flawless skin, a touch of mascara on her eye-lashes, and a faint darkness on the lids which seemed to double the size they were ordinarily.

There was also what Marie called just a *soupçon* of rouge on her cheeks.

When Ingrid had finished using a salve on her lips, Loretta knew that her father would have sent her upstairs immediately to wash her face.

However, Ingrid had been very clever.

It would have been difficult for anyone who did not know Loretta to realise how different she looked when she was herself.

She finally rose from the dressing-table to look in a full-length mirror and she thought that even Christopher would barely recognise her.

At the same time he would immediately want to change her back into her real self.

"Now, Loretta, I want to talk to you alone," Ingrid said.

They left the two maids exclaiming at how beautiful she looked, and went into Ingrid's *Boudoir* which opened out of her bedroom.

It was a delightfully sunny room, exquisitely furnished.

It struck Loretta that everything in it seemed somehow the right background for love.

She sat down in an armchair covered with *petit-point*.

She knew without being told that Ingrid had created for the Marquess an atmosphere of love from which it was impossible for him to escape.

"They are so happy!" Loretta told herself enviously. "How could I be married without love, knowing that my future life would be lonely, desolate and eventually disastrous."

She therefore forced herself to concentrate very carefully on what Ingrid was saying to her.

"Now dearest, let us go over it, step by step. You are

an English-woman married to a dull and very selfish husband. Because you are unhappy although you are too proud to admit it, you have come to Paris knowing that I am the only one of your friends who would understand how much you are suffering."

Ingrid paused, then with a twinkle in her eyes she asked:

"Does that sound logical to you?"

"I think it would make anyone, unless they had a heart of stone, weep over my plight!" Loretta laughed.

"Good!" Ingrid said. "Now we go on from there, and this is important."

Loretta was listening intently as Ingrid said:

"Because of what you have suffered, you have a dislike of all men. You are suspicious of anything they say to you, and have no intention of becoming involved in any way with any men who try to flirt with you."

She thought Loretta looked puzzled and she explained:

"You do see, dearest, unless you are to appear fast and frivolous, you have to make it very clear that you do not want an *affaire de coeur* unlike the majority of women who come to Paris for just that sort of amusement."

"No, of course not!"

"That is why you hold yourself proudly and make yourself out to be a cold woman, disillusioned by life, with no intention of having your affections engaged by a man who, like your husband, will become quickly bored with you."

Loretta laughed.

"I understand exactly what you are saying. You think the *Marquis* may attempt to flirt with me, and I must make it very clear he does not interest me."

"That is very important," Ingrid insisted. "I want you to see him, I want you to talk to him, but on no account must you get embroiled with him in any way."

She smiled and then went on:

63

"I am sure that although he will obviously think you beautiful, he will find any woman who is not interested in him personally not worth his attention."

Loretta clapped her hands together.

"Ingrid, you are a genius! I can understand the complexities of the situation and I will make it very clear to *Monsieur Casanova* that I do not find him attractive as a man, and I am only being polite because he is your guest."

"That is exactly what you have to do," Ingrid said, "and promise me, promise me faithfully, Loretta, that you will not be beguiled by Fabian! I warn you he is a 'Pied Piper' where women are concerned and, whatever tune he plays, they follow him!"

"Do not worry!" Loretta said. "I shall be thinking all the time that if he marries me as Papa intends, I shall be sitting alone in some dismal *château* in France where I know nobody, while my husband is pursuing the beautiful women of Paris."

"That is exactly what he will do," Ingrid said, "so do not listen to the delightful things he will say to you. Do not be deceived by his flattery, which can be very eloquent, and remember that everything he says to you he has said a hundred times before to hundreds of stupid enamoured women who are now weeping their eyes out because he is no longer interested in them."

"He sounds abominable!" Loretta cried. "Do not worry about me, Ingrid. 'Forewarned is forearmed!' and I think my Guardian Angel must have told me to come to you after Papa made it absolutely clear that I had no choice but to marry the *Marquis*."

"Egged on, of course, by the *Duc!*" Ingrid added. "But do not forget that the *Marquis* is enamoured of *Madame* Julie St. Gervaise."

"Is that the name of the lady whom he might marry?"

"I said it was possible for him to do so, but if you ask me, I think Fabian has made up his mind never to marry again, and he will fight desperately to keep his freedom."

"I hope you are right," Loretta said, "in which case it will be easier for me."

"Yes, of course," Ingrid agreed, "but you must not count on it. You have to play the part very skilfully, and to remember that because you are here in this house he will think perhaps you are . . ."

She paused for a moment, then obviously changing what she had been about to say, went on:

". . . not as respectable as our – relatives."

Loretta was not quite certain what she meant, but said:

"I will behave in exactly the same way as Aunt Edith used to do when she disapproved of something you had said when you stayed with us at home."

Ingrid burst out laughing.

"I remember how she was continually telling your father I was a bad influence on you, and of course predicted to all and sundry that I would come to a sticky end! Which I am sure she is still saying in Heaven, or wherever she may be!"

Because it sounded so funny Loretta laughed too.

They were both still reminiscing over their relatives when the Marquess sent a message to say that Ingrid should come downstairs because her guests soon would be arriving.

"Is it a . . big party?" Loretta asked a little nervously.

"No, only half-a-dozen men."

"Only men?" Loretta questioned. "I did not see any women at your party last night."

Ingrid looked at her in a rather strange way.

"Surely you understand why?"

Loretta shook her head.

"Then let me explain," Ingrid said, "that as far as women or rather what you and I call 'Ladies' are concerned, I am 'beyond the pale' – a scarlet woman whom they pass by with their heads averted in case I should contaminate them."

She drew in her breath and continued:

"But because I want Hugh to be happy, I have deliberately encouraged the most interesting, intelligent men in Paris to come here for parties, and small luncheons, like we are having today."

She looked at Loretta to see if she understood and went on:

"Hugh is a very intelligent man, and I have made sure by providing his friends, whoever they may be, with the best food and drink, and by keeping the conversation on a very high intellectual level, that we now have, although it seems incredible, what the French call a 'Salon'."

"It sounds fascinating," Loretta added.

"Some artists and musicians are among those who are welcome," Ingrid went on, "and occasionally, just occasionally, we have women guests who themselves are not accepted by the more particular French hostesses, but who are talented and have exceptional personalities of their own."

She paused and said with a smile:

"Otherwise our guests are always male, and I find it fascinating and intriguing to entertain men who hold important posts in the Government or who are famed in some field or another for the brilliance of their intellect."

"I think it is wonderful!" Loretta said. "Now I understand why the Marquess will never leave you, however many years it may be before you can be married."

"That is what I pray for every night of my life," Ingrid said simply. "I love Hugh, I would die for him; but, what is more difficult, I am determined his life shall be so happy that he will never have even one regret."

"I am sure that is what you are achieving," Loretta said and kissed Ingrid.

66

Ingrid, after a quick look at herself in the mirror, hurried downstairs.

"Wait exactly ten minutes," she said, "then come to the Silver Salon which is where we are meeting before luncheon. The servants in the hall will tell you where it is."

Loretta smiled at her.

"Are you suggesting I make an entrance?" she asked.

"Of course!" Ingrid replied. "I want to make sure you are the sensation you will be, and that all the gentlemen present will be bowled over by your beauty."

"Now you are frightening me."

"Enjoy their compliments, but remember Fabian is dangerous!"

As her cousin walked towards the door Loretta said:

"Thank you, darling Ingrid, and I do hope I shall not let you down."

"Just keep thinking of those two old gentlemen plotting together to marry their children off, whether they like it or not, and I am sure you will have no difficulty in playing your part very plausibly," Ingrid replied.

Then as she smiled at her she left the room and Loretta was alone.

She went to the mantelpiece to look at herself in the mirror that hung above it.

For the moment all she could see was her own eyes wide and a little frightened.

She took in the elaborate new coiffure that Ingrid's maid had given her!

She saw how the Paris gown she was wearing accentuated the curves of her breasts and made her waist seem impossibly tiny.

Then she told herself firmly:

"I am English, cold, disdainful, very suspicious of men, and especially of Frenchmen!"

Suddenly with an exclamation of horror, she remembered although she and Ingrid had talked so much they had not decided what her name should be.

She was wondering desperately what she could do about it, when the door opened.

A footman crossed the room to hand her a note resting on a silver salver.

She took it from him.

She knew, just as she had suddenly realised that vital omission in their plans, so Ingrid had realised it too.

As she took the note in her hand she saw it was addressed to: '*Lady Brompton*' and opening the envelope she saw one word was written on a piece of paper – Lora.

The footman left the room and Loretta smiled to herself.

"That is a clever name, very English, quite ordinary. Not at all the sort of name which would immediately make anyone, especially a foreigner, connect it with anyone of importance."

"I am Lady Brompton!" Loretta informed her reflection in the mirror.

She knew, as she glanced at the hands of the marble clock facing her, it was time to go downstairs.

A footman was waiting for her in the hall, and when she asked him to take her to the Silver Salon he went ahead of her to open a door.

For a moment, as Loretta entered the room she had not seen before, everything seemed to swim in front of her.

Then she saw Ingrid, looking like a flower as she stood surrounded by the gentlemen in their dark clothes, and walked slowly across the Aubusson carpet towards her.

For a moment it seemed as if Ingrid had not noticed her. Then giving a cry of delight she said:

"Good-morning, dearest! I do hope you had a good night!"

"I slept peacefully," Loretta replied, "but I am afraid rather late."

"You are punctual for luncheon, which is all that matters," Ingrid remarked, "and now I must introduce you to my guests."

"I think first," the Marquess interrupted, "Lady Brompton should have a glass of champagne to sweep away the cobwebs of her journey."

There was a twinkle in his eyes as he spoke.

Loretta was aware that Ingrid had rehearsed him also as to how he was to behave and who she was supposed to be.

"May I say how charming your house is!" Loretta said conversationally as she took the glass of champagne from the Marquess's hand. "I was too tired last night to take everything in, but now I see you have a collection of treasures which I am longing to examine more closely."

"You shall see them all," the Marquess promised.

Then Ingrid was saying:

"Let me introduce to you *le Comte* . . ."

Because Loretta, despite what she thought was an excellent piece of acting, was really feeling rather frightened, she did not hear the names of the gentlemen in the room.

She was introduced one after the other, until finally Ingrid said:

"The *Marquis de* Sauerdun! And let me warn you not to believe a single word he says!"

"I never expected you would be so unkind to me!" a deep voice replied.

There was a touch of amusement in it, as if he knew perceptively that Ingrid had some reason for what she said.

Loretta lifted her eyes to the *Marquis* as perfunctorily he raised her hand to his lips.

She did not know exactly what she had expected.

Certainly not a man who looked so unusual, and yet at the same time so compellingly handsome and masculine.

Now she could understand exactly what Ingrid had been trying to explain to her.

It was difficult to describe, even to herself, why he seemed different from every other man in the room.

There was something raffish about him, there was something too, which made him seem overwhelming and in some strange way dominating.

It was as if he was a god who had stepped down from another world to mix with the human beings on this one.

He looked into her eyes and she was conscious of the strength of his fingers as he held her hand.

A magnetic vibration seemed to link her to him and made her afraid.

For a moment she could only stare at him.

Then with what demanded almost a superhuman effort she looked away.

The *Marquis* said softly:

"I am enchanted, *Madame*, and I have a feeling which I cannot explain that this is an important moment in my life!"

Loretta drew in her breath.

Taking her hand away from his, she managed to say in what she hoped was a cold, rather aloof voice:

"It is important to me, *Monsieur* because this is the first time I have been to Paris, and everything in consequence will I am sure be very memorable."

She wanted to move away as she finished speaking.

Somehow, because Ingrid had taken her through the other guests to meet the *Marquis* last, she felt as if they were isolated together and everybody else had receded into the background.

"Your first time in Paris!" the *Marquis* repeated. "Then

70

naturally, you must allow me to make sure it is a milestone in your life and completely unforgettable."

They were speaking in French.

Because his voice was so deep and resonant, it made Loretta feel as if they spoke to music.

Then as she turned her eyes away from his, he said quietly:

"You are very beautiful, more beautiful than I imagined anyone could be!"

For a moment Loretta was beguiled by his words, the tone of his voice and the strange magnetism which was still holding her as if she was his captive.

Then with an effort she managed to reply:

"I wonder, *Monsieur*, to how many women you have said those very words, and how many have been foolish enough to believe you?"

The *Marquis* laughed and it was a very spontaneous sound.

"I might have guessed that Ingrid has been warning you against me," he said. "All I can say is that I hope you will be just enough to believe that I am innocent until proved guilty."

"From all I have heard, *Monsieur*, although, of course I may be wrong, there is plenty of proof, as you call it, and many witnesses to it."

She thought as she spoke she was being rather daring, but after all they were speaking in French.

What was she saying did not sound half so rude as it would have done had they been speaking in English.

"Do you really listen to gossip, which in most instances comes either from the gutter, or from those who are envious of other people's pleasures?"

"'Pleasure' is a difficult word to define," Loretta said. "To some it may mean joy and laughter, to others it may mean a fleeting amusement which so often leaves those who have taken part in it hurt and unhappy!"

"I know exactly what you are saying to me, Lady Brompton," the *Marquis* said, "and I know only too well the type of tale with which you have been regaled."

He paused a moment and then went on:

"I am suggesting that as a newcomer to Paris you should enjoy the present while you are here, and remember that the past does not concern you."

He spoke as it seemed quite seriously.

Loretta looked at him in surprise, intending to say something a little scathing.

Also as Ingrid had instructed her, she tried to appear cold, aloof, and if possible, shocked by him.

Instead, as their eyes met again, she found herself tongue-tied.

Besides which, in a way she could not explain, she was quivering a little because of the expression in his eyes.

Then he said in a low voice:

"Although you may not be aware of it, you have offered me a challenge, and one that I cannot possibly resist."

"I do not know what you mean," Loretta replied.

"I think you do," he answered, "and because I intend to show you Paris, and to prove to you that you are wrong, all I wish to know is when you will allow me to escort you?"

# CHAPTER FOUR

The *Marquis* called for Loretta at eight o'clock.

Although she had a feeling she was being foolish, she was waiting extremely excitedly for him to take her out to dinner.

When Ingrid heard that he had invited her, she exclaimed:

"I thought he was being very attentive at luncheon, but are you really wise to go on with this masquerade? After all you have now seen him and you know what he is like. Surely that is enough?"

Loretta knew as she spoke that her cousin was very apprehensive.

Having seen the *Marquis*, she could now understand so much better than she had before why Ingrid was worried about her.

At luncheon she had, as the only other lady present, been seated on the Marquess's right.

Since Fabian de Sauerdun was on his left, she was facing him across the table.

As she sat down she was very conscious that one of the things which made him so different from other men was that there appeared to be an expression of laughter in his eyes.

It was as if he found the world an amusing place.

But the twist of his lips told her too that he was mocking at it.

She found it hard not to stare at him, and turned to the gentleman on her other side.

She learned as luncheon continued he was the *Comte* Eugene de Marais.

He was a little older, perhaps nearing forty, and he immediately flirted with her in exactly the way she expected.

Creating in everything he said an innuendo, and paying her compliments so extravagant that, instead of feeling shy, she was merely amused by them.

At the same time she was aware that the conversation all round the table was exceedingly interesting.

She was pleased that she could understand nearly everything the gentlemen were discussing.

Her father although he seldom listened to anyone, was an intelligent man.

He had a habit of discussing and criticising at meal-times what had appeared in the newspapers that morning.

Loretta therefore had a comprehension of the political situation in France.

She knew of the scandal that had just caused the fall of the Prime Minister Rouvier and the resignation of the President Jules Grévy, when it was found his son-in-law had been trafficking in decorations and particularly in the much-coveted *Légion d'Honneur.*

Because she was able to join in and make intelligent comments on what was being said, she thought Ingrid looked at her with approval.

Yet she was surprised when the *Marquis* said across the table:

"Is it possible that you are clever as well as beautiful? It is unfair for a mere man to have to cope with such a combination!"

Loretta laughed. Then she said:

"As you are well aware, *Monsieur*, I am only a humble pupil sitting at the feet of the great masters."

"I am sure any gentleman here would be flattered to hear himself described in such a way," the *Marquis* said mockingly.

But Loretta was following her own thoughts and she said:

"It must be the way in which the Ancient Greeks talked amongst themselves and in consequence taught the civilised world to think."

The *Marquis* looked at her for explanation, then he exclaimed:

"Of course! Now I know what was eluding me when I first saw you. It is that you are a Greek, not from Athens, but rather from Mount Olympus."

Loretta wanted to laugh because she was sure he must have said this before to many women. It sounded as if it came too easily to his lips.

And yet there did seem a sincerity about him, though she told herself scornfully it was all part of the act.

Remembering how Ingrid had told her to behave, she tried to look at him coldly.

Without answering what he said she started to talk to the Marquess about the fear of a revolution on which her father had been very eloquent.

"I think it unlikely that anything quite so explosive will happen," the Marquess said. "France is growing more prosperous and more bourgeois, and there is much less poverty than there was in the past."

"I cannot understand," the *Marquis* interrupted, "why Lady Brompton should worry her head with our problems, unless of course she is one of those ardent reformers who always wish to interfere in other people's affairs and forget their own."

Before Loretta, trying to think of some rather stinging retort, could answer, the *Comte* on her other side said:

"As far as I am concerned, Lady Brompton can interfere in as many of my problems as she likes! All I want is to make sure she does not forget me."

He spoke as if he supposed that such a thing was impossible.

Because Loretta wanted to show the *Marquis* she was not interested in him, she said with a sweet smile:

"I assure you, *Monsieur*, I should find it very difficult to forget anyone who can say such charming things to me."

She thought as she spoke that perhaps this was a little out of character with her supposed dislike of men.

So she stiffened and became silent for a while.

In fact, she found it fascinating to listen to the discussions and arguments being conducted.

She guessed that Ingrid had been clever enough to have a narrow dining-table so that her guests found it just as easy to talk across it as to their immediate neighbours.

She was to learn now and have confirmation later that French men when discussing politics always wanted to speak as if they were on a platform and hold everybody else attentively silent.

The whole atmosphere was so different from the rather stiff luncheons and dinner-parties which she had experienced at home.

Despite herself, Loretta could not help becoming animated and joining in eagerly on any subjects which were familiar to her.

When they moved from the Dining Room the *Marquis* came to her side to say:

"You did promise me, Lady Brompton, that you would let me show you Paris. I suggest we start by seeing how beautiful it is by night."

Loretta looked at him in surprise, and he went on:

"I will take you to dine in a place that is essentially

French, where you will have the best food in Paris, and afterwards we will drive along the Seine."

He smiled at her.

"It is a sight you should see also in the daytime, but I think you will agree with me there is nothing more beautiful or romantic than the river at night."

For a moment Loretta hesitated.

She was thinking that to dine alone with a man was something she should certainly not do.

Then she remembered she was a married woman, and she had heard that in France, unlike England, it was possible for a lady to dine in a Restaurant.

Especially when she was flaunting the conventions by staying with Ingrid.

"I will not take 'no' for an answer," the *Marquis* said before she could speak. "So do not, Lady Brompton, make me go down on my knees to persuade you to accept my invitation."

"There is no need for you to do anything so exaggerated or theatrical," Loretta said coolly, "as I have no previous engagements, having only just arrived in Paris, I should be delighted, *Monsieur*, to accept your kind invitation."

"Thank you! I am very conscious of how privileged I am."

He spoke in the same quiet, calm manner as she had.

She was aware as he did so that his eyes were twinkling and she knew that actually he was laughing at her.

It was then that Ingrid came up to them and said:

"Did I hear you inviting my friend Lora to dine with you this evening, Fabian?"

"I have asked her, and she has accepted," the *Marquis* replied.

"Then I beg you to be very careful not to upset her."

"Why should I do that?"

"You know exactly what I mean," Ingrid said. "She

has come to me because she needs my help and advice, and I can only say that you are not the right person, certainly not one I would choose, to assist her at this particular moment."

"Now you are being unkind to me again," the *Marquis* protested. "What have I done to get into your bad books?"

"You know that Hugh and I are very fond of you, Fabian," Ingrid answered, "and we accept you as you are. But I feel I ought to protect my friend from you, simply because living quietly in England she has never met anyone like you before."

"If Lady Brompton has any complaints to make about me, then I will apologise and make restitution," the *Marquis* said, "but I cannot really be contrite for sins I have not yet committed!"

He bent over Ingrid's hand as he spoke.

*"Au revoir,"* he said, "and thank you for another delightful luncheon."

He then took Loretta's hand in his, and once again she was acutely conscious of the vibrations emanating from him as he looked into her eyes and said quietly:

"Until tonight, and I promise that you will not be disappointed."

He walked away, and she thought as she looked after him that with his square shoulders tapering down to narrow hips he looked very athletic and at the same time more elegant than any other man in the room.

As soon as the last guest had gone Ingrid said:

"Now, if you are to dine with Fabian tonight, we must hurry. You will need a new gown and one which will give you confidence."

"Do you think that is what I will need?" Loretta enquired.

"You have to steel yourself against not only what he says, but the way he will exude a personal magic which, as I have already told you, no woman can resist."

Loretta thought of the magnetism she had felt coming from the *Marquis* and knew what Ingrid was saying was the truth.

She hoped that a new gown would help her to think herself more securely into the part she had to play.

She would, at the same time, gain enough evidence about the *Marquis* with which to confound her father and convince him that he would be an impossible husband.

"There are two great Fashion Houses in France, as I expect you are aware," Ingrid was saying, "Worth and Laferrière. I think on the whole, Laferrière will suit you better than the more famous and rather spoilt Frederick Worth."

When later they returned from the Rue de la Paix to the Champs Élysées, Loretta was ready to agree.

Nobody could have made her look more sophisticated, more French, and more *chic* than Laferrière.

She had intended to buy only one evening-gown.

Ingrid insisted on her purchasing three, and also several very elegant day-gowns, which were all so becoming that it was impossible to choose between them.

While she was fascinated by clothes that were different from anything she had worn before, Loretta was also listening to everything Ingrid told her about the *Marquis*.

"I suppose in every century there have been a few women who were irresistible to men," she said, "not only because of their beauty, but because of their character and personality, and the same applies to the opposite sex."

She glanced at Loretta as she went on:

"When we refer to Fabian as a 'modern Casanova', or a 'Don Juan', it is, in a way, a compliment because he has something which other men do not have."

"Magnetism!" Loretta said beneath her breath, but Ingrid continued:

79

"No-one could be more delightful, more intelligent, or more charming as a companion, but as a husband he would be very different!"

She put her hand on Loretta as she said gently:

"I am only frightened, my dearest, that despite everything I have said, you will fall in love with Fabian and allow Cousin Arthur to persuade you into marrying a man who will make you more unhappy than you can ever begin to imagine."

"I realise that," Loretta replied. "The only difficulty is to find out something substantial against him that will persuade Papa that I am not just a stupid young girl, shocked because a man has had a number of love-affairs before he takes a wife."

"Only the English believe that a Rake can be reformed," Ingrid said sarcastically. "The French have learnt that 'a leopard never changes his spots'. A Frenchwoman therefore expects her husband to be unfaithful, and it comes as no surprise to her when he is."

"That must make her very unhappy."

"I suppose it does," Ingrid agreed. "At the same time, as the marriage is arranged and takes place when the man and woman are still quite young, it is doubtful if she knows what love is, or what she is missing, until she is much older."

Loretta knew that she too was still young, and yet she was thinking of the idealistic love which a man like the *Marquis* would never give her.

Ingrid had not found it until after her marriage.

Both she and the Marquess had made great sacrifices rather than lose it.

'That is the love I want,' she thought as she had thought ever since she had come to Paris.

It was impossible to see Ingrid and the Marquess together without knowing they vibrated to each other.

She had been aware at luncheon that the Marquess's

eyes kept going down the table to where Ingrid was sitting at the end of it.

There was an expression on his face that Loretta knew was very different from the way the *Comte de* Marais was looking flirtatiously at her.

During luncheon he had said in a low voice:

"I have to see you again, *Madame*. I have a great deal to say to you, and we must be alone."

There was something about the way he spoke, and her instinctive feeling that he was intruding on her, which made Loretta wish to move away from him.

It struck her that he was in fact quite repulsive, and she disliked the caressing note in his voice.

When he put out his hand to touch her before they left the table, it made her feel as if she had been touched by a reptile, something which made her shudder.

She did not answer his request to see her alone, but merely turned away as if she had not heard what he said.

As she did so he gave a low chuckle as if he was amused by her effort to avoid him.

Now as they drove back from their shopping through the Place de la Concorde, she said to Ingrid:

"You may be nervous because I am dining with the *Marquis* this evening, which is something I want to do, but I am very glad indeed I do not have to deal with the *Comte*."

"I agree with you. He is a rather sinister man," Ingrid replied, "a womaniser, and a success with most women. Needless to say, he is jealous of Fabian, and they have on one occasion fought a duel."

"Fought a duel!" Loretta exclaimed. "But surely that is something which is out of fashion and does not take place nowadays."

"That is true of England, but duels are still quite frequent in Paris. They take place traditionally in the Bois, just as they have for a hundred years."

"It seems very uncivilised," Loretta remarked, "and I hope nobody ever fights a duel over me."

"You must not allow them to do so," Ingrid said quickly. "But I warn you not to play the *Comte* off against Fabian, or they will undoubtedly 'call each other out'."

"I hope not to see the *Comte* again."

Loretta spoke too soon.

When they arrived back a servant informed Ingrid that the *Comte* Eugène de Marais was waiting for them in the Silver Salon.

"Now see what you have done!" Ingrid said. "I can think of no reason why Eugène Marais should come here twice in the same day – unless it is to see you."

"Then tell him I have gone upstairs to rest," Loretta said quickly, and without waiting for Ingrid to agree she ran up the stairs to her bedroom.

She did rest before dinner, but it was not for long.

She wanted to take a great deal of trouble in arraying herself in her new gown.

She also wanted to make sure that her cousin put the finishing touches to her face to make her look older and not in the least like a *jeune fille*.

"You look lovely, dearest," Ingrid said when she had finished. "Much, much too lovely. Promise me you will be careful!"

"You are fussing over me like a mother hen with only one chick!" Loretta teased. "I promise you, I can look after myself."

"Touch wood!" Ingrid said quickly. "And remember, it is quite easy to put the Channel between yourself and Fabian."

"I have not forgotten, but I keep remembering also that he will cross it when he accepts Papa's invitation."

When a footman announced that the *Marquis de*

Sauerdun had called for her, she went slowly down the stairs.

She was conscious that her new gown with its train floating behind her like a small wave gave her a dignity which would not have been expected in a young girl.

Her hair was also arranged in a new style.

Not in the rather ugly knot, which was the fashion in England, but it was closely swathed around her head.

It gave her, she thought, the Grecian look to which the *Marquis* had referred at luncheon.

She had not expected him to notice it, but as they drove away in his carriage, he turned sideways to look at her and said:

"Perfect! It is quite obvious tonight that you belong to Olympus and are very much aware of it."

She raised her eyebrows as if she asked for explanation and he said:

"Now not only your nose is Greek, but also your hair, and may I say, and I want you to believe me, that I had no idea any woman could look so lovely!"

Again there was that note of sincerity in his voice which Loretta told herself was all part of his act.

Yet, if he was acting, he was a very skilful performer.

"Where are we dining?" she asked to change the subject away from herself.

"Because I do not want to be disturbed by friends and acquaintances who will be bound to come and talk to me, if only because they are curious to learn who you are, I am taking you to Lapérouse. It is by the Seine and is a small place where we can feel almost as if we are alone."

"It will be the first time I have ever dined in a Restaurant," Loretta confessed.

"I was sure that would be true," the *Marquis* said, "and there are so many other places where I want to take you, Lora. I shall find that more fascinating than it is possible to say in words."

She did not know what he meant and after a moment she said:

"My name is Lady Brompton!"

"It is too late for such formalities!" the *Marquis* replied. "I think you were aware, as I was, when we met today that we recognised each other across time and space."

Loretta looked at him swiftly, then away again before she said:

"H . . how can you . . say such . . things."

She knew as she spoke that strangely enough it was indeed what she had felt.

She had been vividly conscious of his magnetism.

She thought now, although of course it could not be true, that his face which she had to admit fascinated her, could fit onto her dream-man, who until now had been faceless.

Then she told herself she was crazy and this was just the way she must not think. She must remember instead all that Ingrid had said to her.

It was only a short distance to the Restaurant where they were dining.

It was in a tall house and, when they climbed the narrow stairs, they were shown into a small room in which there were only three tables for two, all of them empty.

They were given the best table, which was the one in the window and through it they could see the Seine with the lights reflected in it.

Yet there were also deep shadows which to Loretta seemed filled at the moment with questions turning over and over in her mind.

A waiter brought her a menu, but without looking at it Loretta said to the *Marquis*:

"Will you order for me? I have always heard of the specialities that are obtainable in French Restaurants, but I would not know how to ask for them."

84

"I know your taste," the *Marquis* said, "without your having to explain it to me."

She thought this was a strange thing for him to say.

Yet she had the uncomfortable feeling it was the truth, and that he was aware of what she wanted not only to eat but also to drink.

"This is how he makes every woman he is with feel," she told herself.

Yet it was impossible not to be aware of his vitality as he sat at the other side of the small table, and even harder to prevent herself from staring at him.

He took a long time in choosing what they should eat.

Then a bottle of champagne was ordered, and as Loretta took a sip from her glass she realised that it was finer than any champagne she had ever tasted before.

She continued to look out of the window, because although she fought against it, she felt shy.

However, the *Marquis*, instead of saying anything complimentary, as she had expected, or speaking in the way he had in the carriage, now said conversationally:

"I expect you realise that electricity has given Paris an added splendour. It is now known as '*La Ville Lumière*', and that is why I want you to see '*la fée électricité*', as it is nicknamed, and I know you will admire it."

"I am already fascinated by Paris!" Loretta replied in the same way that he had spoken to her. "I had no idea that the Champs-Élysées was so green and picturesque, and surely, Paris must be the only Capital City where the great private mansions, like that of the Marquess, are sheltered amongst the trees?"

"You are right," the *Marquis* said, "for although London has an atmosphere and attraction all its own, I do not believe any City could be more beautiful than Paris!"

"You know London?"

As she asked the question, she realised that her father

85

had never spoken of the *Marquis* being in England. He often referred after various race-meetings to having met the *Duc* there.

"Yes, I know London quite well," the *Marquis* said, "and of course I am an admirer of its women, who I concede are the most beautiful in the world!"

He paused for a moment before he said:

"It is strange that I have not seen you at any of the Balls I have attended."

"I .. I live very quietly in the .. country," Loretta explained.

"Does that bore you?"

"No, I love the country. I would hate living permanently in a City, even one as beautiful as Paris. I ride, and there are dozens of things to occupy every minute of the day."

"What about the nights?"

Loretta looked at him enquiringly and as she realised what he meant she felt the colour come into her cheeks.

She looked away from him out of the window at the river.

"Have I shocked you?" the *Marquis* asked.

"I am not .. shocked," Loretta managed to reply. "It is just that I consider it in bad taste to speak of .. anything so .. intimate!"

She thought she sounded crushing, but the *Marquis* merely laughed.

"My dear," he said, "I find everything about you so alluring, so different from anybody I have ever known before, that I am captivated by you in a way that is difficult to put into words."

Loretta drew herself up, hoping she looked, as she told Ingrid, like her Aunt Edith.

"I think, *Monsieur*, we should talk about Paris!"

"But I have every intention," the *Marquis* contradicted, "of talking about you."

"It would be more interesting for me if you would talk about yourself."

"Why not?" he enquired. "What do you want to know?"

Loretta hesitated for a moment. Then she asked:

"I can hardly believe that when you invited me to dine with you tonight you had not already an engagement with somebody else."

She paused, then hoping to surprise him she said:

"Somebody who has been left unhappy because you have altered your engagements."

"I think the right word for it is that I changed my direction," the *Marquis* said. "Of course I was not going to sit at home all the evening by myself reading the newspapers! But nothing was more important, Lora, than being with you!"

"That sounds plausible," Loretta said, "at the same time, it bears out your reputation."

"My reputation for what?"

"Of being cruel and unkind to those for whom you have no further use."

The *Marquis*'s lips twisted in a mocking manner that she found fascinating before he replied:

"Again you are probing into the past, and I have told you to think of the present and the future."

"Tomorrow I shall be the past," Loretta replied, "and I have no intention of crying over it."

"We are fencing with words," the *Marquis* answered. "You will always be my present and my future. Our past is not yesterday or the day before, but perhaps a thousand years earlier when, as you said at luncheon, we met in Athens or on Mount Olympus."

"I did not say I met you!"

"But that is what you were thinking," the *Marquis* said, "and I was thinking exactly the same. It is something we cannot argue about because it definitely happened, and ever since then I have been searching for you."

Because of the quiet way he spoke and because again there was a note of sincerity in his voice that made it impossible for her to know how to refute him, Loretta said quickly:

"You are breaking your promise."

"What promise?"

"That you would show me Paris."

"That is what I intend to do, but there is no hurry. We have this evening and the rest of our lives in front of us, so it is easier to talk about ourselves."

"It is not easy for me," Loretta objected, "and anyway, I do not understand what you are saying."

"That is not true," the *Marquis* contradicted. "You understand me perfectly, just as I understand you. There is no need for words. We have only to sit here and feel we are joined by an invisible force which neither of us can resist."

Loretta drew in her breath.

She felt, although he had not moved, that he was holding her, drawing her closer.

That she was becoming merged into him in a way that made her lose her own identity and become part of his.

For a moment they did not speak, she only raised her eyes and there was an appeal in them he understood.

"I will not frighten you," he said caressingly, "for that is something I have no wish to do."

He smiled at her and then went on:

"If it makes you happy, I will tell you what you think you want to hear, but is really quite unimportant beside the fact that we are together."

Then with an irresistible charm he began to talk of Paris.

He talked not only of the new Paris of Baron

Houssmann but the people he knew and who he would like Loretta to meet.

He told her of the old *Princesse* de Metternich, who, after leading a life of pleasure had turned to art and had become a passionate Wagnerite.

She was a niece of Napoleon I, and she kept open house for Dandies, painters and writers.

"It was just the sort of *Salon*," he said, "which your friend Ingrid is creating and which I think in the future will be one of the most important meeting places in Paris."

"Do you really think that?" Loretta asked. "I do want Ingrid to be happy."

There was no need to explain, and the *Marquis* said:

"She may not be accepted by the families of the *ancien régime* who live only in the past, but she will keep Hugh Galston happy, by making him part of what is now more important than the Social World, the new aristocracy of intellect and power which no man can resist."

"I am glad you should say that," Loretta cried. "It is what I want for both of them."

"It is what they will have," the *Marquis* said, "and it is what they deserve, having had the courage to admit that the love they have for each other is more valuable than anything else in the world."

"You really believe that?"

"I believe it. It is what I want, and it is what you want," he said, "and therefore as we have found it, we will have to show the same bravery as Ingrid and Hugh have shown."

He spoke very solemnly, and Loretta felt although she tried to prevent it, her whole being respond to what he was saying.

It was a relief when the waiter interrupted with the first course.

They ate a delicious meal and when they left the

Restaurant it was to find that the *Marquis*'s carriage had been opened.

"Now I can see the lights of Paris," Loretta exclaimed in delight.

They drove beside the Seine.

She looked at the lighted barges and occasionally the *bateaux-mouches* gaily decorated with pennants and streamers, obviously coming back from some citizen's outing.

She thought that nothing could be more lovely or attractive.

The chestnut trees that bordered the road were in bloom, the air seeming scented with their fragrance, and as they drove along she was continually hearing the sounds of music in the distance.

It was all so fascinating, and yet all the time she was aware that the *Marquis* was not looking at the lights, as she was, but at her.

He did not attempt to touch her.

In fact, he sat as far away from her as it was possible to do.

Yet she felt that they were so near and so close to each other that it was an intimacy she had never known before.

The coachman obviously had his instructions.

They drove until she realised they were now in the Bois de Boulogne, with the trees overhead.

The stars shining through them made it even more romantic than the lights of the City.

They drove for some way, when the carriage came to a standstill and the *Marquis* said:

"I want you to alight as I have something to show you."

Loretta felt nervous.

"Perhaps that . . would be a . . mistake," she said in a low voice.

"There is nothing to make you afraid," he said quietly, "and it is only a very short distance to walk."

It was impossible to insist in remaining in the carriage.

As Loretta stepped out she found that just in front of them was a path leading under the trees towards some lights in the distance.

She walked a little more quickly than was necessary because she felt she was stepping into the unknown.

Then as the light grew brighter she found the *Marquis* had taken her to a cascading fountain, where the concealed lights in its stone basin turned the water flashing up into the darkness of the sky into a thousand iridescent rainbows.

It was so lovely that Loretta stood staring at it in delight, her eyes shining, her lips parted a little.

Then after some moments of silence the *Marquis* said:

"Look at me, Lora, I want you to look at me."

Loretta turned her face slowly, feeling she had been swept away into the sky by the beauty of the fountain and now he was bringing her back to earth.

Then as she looked up at him she felt although he had not moved that he held her prisoner, and her eyes could not leave his.

"I brought you here tonight," he said very quietly, "because I intended to kiss you, as I have wanted to do ever since I first saw you."

Loretta gave a little murmur of dissent as he went on:

"But now I am not going to touch you, because I want you to think of me as I believe you do already, as somebody very different from the men who have pursued you, and naturally made love to you in the past."

Loretta's eyes widened, but she did not speak and the *Marquis* said:

"There is an aura about you, my darling, which protects you, and I can only pray that it is not only from me, but from anyone else who may come near you."

His voice grew deeper as he went on:

"But because I want you to think only of me, because I want you to realise what has happened to us both I am going to take you home, and ask you to dream of me, as I shall be dreaming of you."

Loretta could not help thinking as he spoke that she had dreamed of him for a long time.

Then the *Marquis* took her hand in his, and she felt his lips gentle and insistent on the softness of her skin.

He held them there for a moment, then as if he could not help himself, he turned her hand over and pressed his lips against the palm.

It was something Loretta had never thought of a man doing.

It not only surprised her, but at the same time, she was conscious that it sent a quiver through her.

Then she felt as if the beauty of the cascade ran through her body, and there were rainbows within her breasts and touching her lips.

The *Marquis* raised his head and said with an air of authority:

"Now I will take you home!"

He put his hand under her arm and helped her back along the path under the trees to where the carriage was waiting.

He assisted her into it, then went around to the other side so as not to cross in front of her to reach his own seat.

The carriage drove off and soon there were the lights in the streets and the houses and they were back in the City.

The carriage came to a standstill and the *Marquis* stepped out to help Loretta alight and took her up the steps to the front door.

Before the night-footman could open it he said quietly:

"*Bonne nuit*, my beautiful one! I shall see you tomorrow, but remember, before you go to sleep, that I love you!"

Then as the door opened he was gone and Loretta, with his words ringing in her ears, walked into the Hall.

# CHAPTER FIVE

When Loretta awoke in the morning she could hardly believe that last night had not been a dream.

It seemed too extraordinary that, despite Ingrid's warning, she had found the *Marquis* was different in every way from what she had expected and had been led to believe about him.

How could he have spoken to her as he had?

How could he have taken her to the cascade, then brought her away in a manner in which, even though she was innocent and unsophisticated, she knew no other man would have behaved.

"I do not understand," she whispered, "I do not understand him, and why he is as he is."

She longed to ask Ingrid's advice, but she knew it would be impossible to make her cousin or anybody else understand the sensations the *Marquis* aroused in her.

She was also far too shy to repeat anything of what he had said to her.

Her breakfast was brought to her in bed, and afterwards, because she understood from Marie that it was expected, she dressed slowly and did not go downstairs until late in the morning.

There was no sign of Ingrid.

She went into the little Sitting-Room where she had

been taken the first night and sat down to read the newspapers which were full of the excitements that were taking place in Paris.

She had, however, only scanned the headlines when the door opened and a servant said:

"*Monsieur le Comte* de Marais, *Madame!*"

Loretta looked around in dismay.

She had been hoping that the *Marquis* would call, perhaps to take her driving in the Bois.

She had not expected the *Comte* and she thought how tiresomely persistent he was in view of his having called the previous evening.

He came towards her with an expression in his eyes that she disliked, and he raised her hand to his lips far from perfunctorily and actually kissed it.

"Good morning, *Monsieur*," Loretta said in what she hoped was a cold voice. "My hostess did not tell me she was expecting you this morning."

"I called to see you yesterday evening, and you avoided me," the *Comte* replied. "So today I am taking no chances and am asking you, Beautiful Lady, to come driving with me in the Bois, and afterwards we will have luncheon at 'Pre Catelan'."

"It is very kind of you, but unfortunately I have a previous engagement."

"I do not believe it!" he said angrily. "And if it is with Fabian de Sauerdun, I refuse to allow you to go with him!"

Loretta stiffened.

"I do not think, *Monsieur*, that you are in a position of authority over me!"

"That is where you are mistaken," the *Comte* answered. "I claim authority from finding you exquisite, adorable and very, very desirable, and I have no intention of surrendering you to that breaker of hearts, a man whose love affairs are a scandal and a crying disgrace!"

He spoke with such scorn that Loretta wanted to defend the *Marquis* but knew it would be indiscreet.

Instead she said:

"I think, *Monsieur* this conversation is quite uncalled for. I can only thank you for your invitation, but regret I cannot accept it."

"I have already told you that I intend you to have luncheon with me, and also dinner tonight," the *Comte* replied, "and I assure you, my Beautiful, that I always get my own way where a lovely woman is concerned."

He took a step nearer to her as he said:

"When I look at you I know without your telling me that you have never been awakened to the fires of love, to the passion which will make you even more beautiful than you are already."

Loretta felt a repulsion and disgust arise in her simply because he had drawn nearer.

She was also revolted not only by what he was saying, but the way he said it.

She would have moved away had he not reached out to catch hold of her wrist.

"You are driving me crazy!" he exclaimed. "I intend to teach you joys which at the moment you do not know exist."

He would have pulled her to him if Loretta had not given a little cry of protest and tried violently to free her arm from his grip.

"How dare you . . touch me!" she cried angrily.

As the *Comte* gave a little laugh, she knew her resistance excited him, and there was an expression in his eyes which frightened her.

"Let me . . go!"

Then as he relentlessly pulled her nearer and nearer to him and she screamed, the door opened.

It was with a sense of utter relief that Loretta saw Fabian de Sauerdun and the Marquess come into the room.

When they perceived what was occurring they both stood still for a moment, and as the *Comte* released Loretta's wrist she said falteringly, because she was so shaken.

"I was just .. telling *le Comte* .. that I was having .. luncheon with you, *Monsieur le Marquis*."

"Of course," the *Marquis* said without a moment's hesitation. "That is what we arranged, and my Chaise is waiting outside so that we can drive in the Bois before we eat."

Loretta gave a little sigh of relief that the *Marquis* had understood so quickly.

The Marquess walked towards the *Comte* to say:

"Good-morning, Marais! I was not informed of your arrival!"

"I came to see Lady Brompton," the *Comte* replied, "for I had arranged last night to take her out to luncheon."

Because Loretta was frightened she said beneath her breath:

"That .. is not .. true!"

"I am afraid you are too late, Marais," Fabian de Sauerdun said. "My invitation was given first. It is something which seems to happen frequently where we are concerned."

He was being deliberately provocative and the *Comte* stared at him in fury.

"One day I will get even with you, Sauerdun!" he said. "Make no mistake about that!"

The *Marquis* smiled.

"You are surely not suggesting another duel?" he said. "The last one was such a farce that all Paris is still laughing!"

The *Comte* was so incensed that for a moment Loretta was afraid he might even strike the *Marquis*.

Then with an exclamation that was a smothered oath,

he walked from the room, and Loretta feeling quite weak after what had occurred, sat down on the sofa.

"Marais grows more and more intolerable!" the *Marquis* said.

"I agree with you," the Marquess replied, "he is a most unpleasant man, and you certainly must not encourage him, Lora!"

"Of course I did not .. encourage him!" Loretta protested. "He is horrible, repulsive and he .. frightens me!"

"I will make sure he leaves the house," the Marquess said and left the room.

Fabian de Sauerdun sat down beside Loretta on the sofa.

"He shall not frighten you again," he said. "I will protect you from Marais, and any other man like him!"

He saw from the distress on her face and the expression in her eyes that she was greatly upset, and he said quietly and gently without the usual mocking note in his voice:

"Go upstairs and put on your prettiest bonnet. I want all my friends in the Bois to think how lucky I am to have you with me."

Because she knew he was really trying to help her, Loretta gave him a tremulous little smile and rose obediently from the sofa.

When she reached the door it flashed through her mind that perhaps the *Comte* had not yet left.

As if perceptively Fabian knew what she was thinking, he said:

"I will take you to the bottom of the stairs."

As he spoke he put his hand under her arm as he had last night when they left the cascade in the Bois.

She felt he was protecting her, and that it was ridiculous to feel afraid of a man like the *Comte* who could not really hurt her.

"It is only because I am so ignorant of men and the way they behave," Loretta told herself.

She lifted her chin and tried to move in a dignified manner while at the same time she was aware that her heart was still throbbing in her breast.

As they reached the hall it was a relief to see there was no one there except two footmen on duty.

"Do not be long," Fabian said quietly. "I have so much to show you, and the sun is shining."

Once again she flashed him a smile and managed to say: "Thank you for being so kind!" before she ran up the stairs.

She knew as she put on a pretty hat trimmed with white camelias and green leaves, which Ingrid had given her, that it would have been impossible for her not to be upset by a man like the *Comte*.

She had never imagined that any man would behave in such an extraordinary manner, let alone after such a short acquaintance.

It then flashed through her mind that perhaps he could have some excuse, for she had deliberately put herself in a vulnerable position by pretending to be a married woman.

She had further jeopardised her standing by staying with Ingrid, which was something that none of her relatives if aware of it, would have allowed.

"I should go back to England," she told herself.

She knew, however, that was not what she wanted.

She wanted to be with the *Marquis*, not, if she was honest, because she was still trying to find out how really despicable he was and thus have good reason for refusing to marry him, but because she found everything about him fascinating and unusual.

"I have been . . warned! I have been warned!" she told herself as she went down the stairs.

Yet she knew there was an irrepressible excitement running through her as she went back to the Sitting-Room where he was talking to the Marquess.

Both men rose to their feet as she entered and the Marquess said:

"What time shall I tell Ingrid you will be back?"

Loretta looked at Fabian and he said:

"I will bring her back after luncheon, about three o'clock, but I will collect her again at eight, because we are dining at the *Grand Verfour*."

He spoke so positively that Loretta knew there was no question of her arguing about it.

Although she thought the Marquess must be surprised, he merely said:

"The food there is superlative, and I always think it one of the most romantic Restaurants in all Paris."

"So do I," Fabian agreed, but he was looking at Loretta as he spoke.

They drove away behind two perfectly-matched jet-black horses.

Loretta thought it would be impossible for anyone to produce a smarter turn-out even though she had heard her father say that the carriages and riders in the Bois were nothing but a Fashion Parade.

She thought he was right when she saw the elegance of the *Amazones*, as Fabian termed them.

The aristocratic Dandies vied with each other in having the finest horses and most spectacular vehicles.

Loretta and Fabian did not talk very much, but he pointed out to her where duels were fought and added:

"As I expect you can guess, more amorous intrigues take place in the Bois than anywhere else in Paris."

It certainly was, Loretta agreed, exceedingly romantic.

When they stopped at *Pre Catalan* she thought it was the most exciting place for luncheon she could ever have imagined.

It was like a country house surrounded by gardens and trees where the guests could sit out on a green lawn, each table covered with a huge brightly-coloured umbrella.

The tables were arranged so discreetly that nothing that was said could be overheard even by the nearest of other guests.

Loretta looked round her with shining eyes.

Then, as if it was inevitable, beautiful women came up to the *Marquis* one after the other to exclaim reproachfully:

"Fabian! You have been neglecting me! When are you coming to see me?"

There was no doubt they were genuinely eager for him to do so, and Loretta could not help admiring the adroit way in which he answered without committing himself to any positive engagement.

Then when at last it seemed he had spoken to all his friends who were already having luncheon there, he said:

"Now you understand why last night I took you somewhere where we could talk without being interrupted, and that is what I shall do again tonight."

Loretta did not speak and he continued:

"At the same time, I thought it only fair for you to see why Pre Catalan is one of the sights of Paris and something which on your first visit you should not miss."

"You are being very kind to me," Loretta said without thinking.

"How can I help it?" he asked. "And I think perhaps 'kind' is not the right word, for it would be impossible for me to be anything else to you!"

He watched her for a moment before he asked:

"Did you think of me last night?"

"How could I . . help . . it?" Loretta replied.

Then she told herself severely she was allowing herself to be far too intimate with him, and she should have prevaricated.

But she knew that, if she had done so, he would not have believed her.

"I lay awake," he said quietly, "thanking God that I

had found you at last, and that my pilgrimage, which has been a very long one, is over."

Loretta tried deliberately to misunderstand.

She was, however, saved from making a reply because the waiter arrived with the menu and the champagne which Fabian had already ordered was poured into their glasses.

The food, as was to be expected, was delicious.

At the same time Loretta found it difficult to think of anything but the man sitting opposite her, and not to be aware that his eyes were continually on her face.

"I suppose," he said when luncheon was finished, "that you must have some flaws in you somewhere, just like everybody else, but I have yet to find them."

Loretta laughed.

"Please, do not look too hard. I am very conscious of my own short-comings."

"I wonder what they can be," Fabian ruminated. "I find you so perfect – the way you look, how you speak, what you think – that I cannot believe that anyone, however censorious, could be critical of you."

"Then you do not know my relatives!" Loretta replied. "I can assure you they are critical of everybody and everything, and I am not exempt."

She spoke lightly, but as she looked at Fabian she realised his expression was serious.

"You speak of your relations," he said, "but not of your husband. Tell me about him."

The question was so unexpected that although she tried not to be flustered she felt suddenly tongue-tied and the colour rose in her cheeks.

"He must be a very strange man to allow anyone so exceedingly beautiful as his wife to come to Paris alone," Fabian went on, "to stay with Ingrid in her awkward position, and to permit you to meet men like me, who would be inhuman if they did not speak to you of love."

"I cannot .. discuss it," Loretta managed to say at last.

"Why? Do not tell me it is because you love him, because I know, my beautiful little Lora, that you know little or nothing about love, or about men, for that matter."

"I cannot understand why you should .. assume that I am so .. ignorant," Loretta replied feeling she must somehow stand up for herself.

Fabian laughed very softly.

"You are so young and so unspoiled," he said. "I had forgotten there were women like you in the world, and yet incredible though it seems, you are married!"

"Yes, I am married," Loretta said firmly, "and as I told you before, *Monsieur*, you should not speak to me as you do."

"How can I help it?" Fabian asked. "And how can you help what you feel for me?"

Loretta wanted to say that she felt nothing for him except that he was an interesting stranger.

Then as she looked at him, once again her eyes were held by his and it was impossible to look away.

"My darling, you are so transparent," he said quietly. "I know everything about you, and I know too that I excite you! Even though you will not admit it, your heart is beating a little faster because we are together, and your lips, which I have not yet kissed, are waiting for mine."

What he said seemed to mesmerise Loretta into immobility.

Then with an effort which made her feel as if she had struck herself physically she said:

"I think it is .. time I went .. home."

"That is where I will take you," Fabian said, "and tonight we will continue our conversation where it has left off."

Loretta wanted to say that she would not listen to him, but she knew that was untrue.

She wanted him to go on talking to her in the strange voice which seemed to make little shafts of sunshine run through her body.

She was aware, although she tried not to believe it, that she thrilled to his words and the sincerity with which he seemed to utter them.

'He is a "Pied Piper" as Ingrid told me,' she thought, 'and just like all the other stupid women, I am running after him to destruction!'

She walked ahead of him across the lawn to where his Chaise was waiting under the trees.

As he helped her into it, she told herself again as she felt herself quiver at his touch, that she must leave Paris.

"I am making a fool of myself," she scolded.

Then as he sat beside her and took up the reins, she thought he looked like Apollo driving his horses across the sky.

No one could look more incredibly attractive, or so exciting, and yet he was as despicable as everybody warned her he was.

Fabian drove a longer way around the Bois than was necessary.

He wanted Loretta to see the beauty of the trees, and the flowers, and the boys playing football on an open patch of ground.

A few minutes later they were back in the tree-lined boulevards.

There were people moving slowly along the pavements, or sitting outside the Cafés with the inevitable cup of coffee in front of them.

He drove her back to the Marquess's house.

As a groom ran to the horses' heads, he stepped down to help her alight, saying as he did so:

"*Au revoir* my beautiful little goddess, until tonight."

Loretta stopped at the bottom of the steps.

"If I .. come," she said with an effort, "you must not

. . talk to me . . like that."

"Why not?"

"Because it is . . wrong . . . ." she began.

"There is nothing wrong," Fabian said softly, "in what I feel for you and what you feel for me. We can talk about it until the stars fall from the skies, but we cannot change our hearts, and to deny love, as you well know, is blasphemy."

Again he was being serious.

As he took her hand in his Loretta was vividly conscious of his magnetism reaching out to her, holding her.

She had the frightening feeling there was no escape.

She did not answer him, but merely walked up the steps, and as she did so, he said: "Until eight o'clock," then climbed back into his Chaise.

Ingrid was waiting for her in the hall.

She kissed Loretta and exclaimed:

"I was surprised, dearest, when Hugh told me you were having luncheon with Fabian, and even more surprised when I heard how badly the *Comte* behaved."

"He is a horrible man!" Loretta exclaimed.

"I agree with you. At the same time, he is of great importance in the Financial World, and I want Hugh to be friendly with the 'Kings of Finance', just as I wish him to be *persona grata* with the politicians who rule our lives."

"I understand what you are saying," Loretta replied, in a low voice, "but I am finding it very difficult to be . . polite to the *Comte* when he behaves in such an . . extraordinary manner."

"He believes that every woman is in love with him rather than with his money," Ingrid said.

"And why does he hate the *Marquis?*"

Ingrid laughed.

"Need you ask? It is because they have clashed at various times before over the pursuit of some new beauty, and invariably Fabian has been the winner."

"I do not wish to see the *Comte* again!" Loretta said firmly.

"I will do my best," Ingrid promised, "but it will not be easy!"

Loretta took off her hat, then she said:

"Am I being a nuisance, Ingrid? Would you like me to leave?"

"No, of course not," Ingrid replied. "I love having you here, and it means more than I can possibly say that you have come to me with your problems."

Her voice deepened, and she said:

"I only hope I can help you. If I fail, it will not be for want of trying."

"You have helped me already."

As Loretta spoke she moved restlessly across the room to stand looking out of the window.

"I wish I could be sure of that," Ingrid said behind her. "I have a feeling, although I may be wrong, that you are finding Fabian far more attractive than you thought he would be."

Because that was true, Loretta could only nod her head, and after a moment Ingrid said:

"The strange thing about Fabian is that despite his reputation, despite his success with women, most men, with the exception of the *Comte*, like him and trust him. Hugh, in fact, is devoted to him."

Loretta knew exactly how much this meant.

She was aware that if her father criticised a man and despised him he was invariably right, and the man in question was undesirable.

That Ingrid should speak in such a way about a man against whom she had warned her as a husband, made what she was feeling and thinking even more complex than it was already.

To change the subject she asked:

"Is there anything we have to do this afternoon?"

"More shopping, if that would interest you," Ingrid replied. "Of course there is still a great deal of Paris for you to see, but I am leaving that to Fabian."

"When he brought me back after luncheon, I hoped he might suggest taking me sight-seeing."

"I expect," Ingrid replied, "he is going to play Polo, and did not want to let his side down."

"Polo?" Loretta questioned.

"I thought you knew," Ingrid replied, "that the reason why Fabian is not as interested in race-horses as his father is, is that he is an outstanding Polo player. In fact he is in the top team which represents Paris."

"I had no idea of it," Loretta said. "I did notice that his horses were very fine, but I thought as he never came to the race-meetings in England that he was not particularly interested in them, except as a mode of conveyance."

Ingrid laughed.

"If you said that to Fabian he would have a fit! His own horses, quite apart from his father's, are outstanding, and his stable in Normandy is considered the best in the whole country. He has race-horses, but he is not obsessed by them as is the *Duc*."

"Now I understand why Papa has not met him," Loretta said. "It puzzled me."

"There are many things about Fabian that will puzzle you," Ingrid replied. "It is a pity that he is impossible as a husband, and yet so very eligible in every other way."

They talked of other things, but Loretta found her thoughts continually returning to the *Marquis*.

It was no use pretending, and as she went up to dress before dinner she knew she wanted to be with him, she wanted to talk to him.

When he spoke as he did of their feelings for each other it made her shy.

But he evoked sensations that she dare not admit and

tried not to think about.

'If I feel like this now,' she tried to say to herself severely, 'what would I feel if I married him, and then he left me for another woman?'

It was such an agonising thought that she tried to make herself feel cold and aloof and indifferent as she bathed in the syringa-scented water.

She then put on another of the beautiful gowns that she had bought with Ingrid, at Laferrière.

It was a gown that made her look like a rose.

At the same time there were little touches of velvet among the chiffon and silver where it was least expected, which made it a sophisticated gown.

It would certainly not have been chosen by a débutante.

Because she had no jewels such as a married woman was expected to possess, Ingrid lent her a small diamond necklace from which hung a large, perfect pear-shaped pearl.

There were earrings to match and bracelets to wear over long gloves which were the same colour as her gown.

"You look absolutely lovely!" Ingrid exclaimed when she saw her.

Loretta had gone to her room to say goodnight because Ingrid was dining much later with the Marquess and was therefore resting on a *chaise longue* wearing an exotic *negligée* of green gauze.

"Have an enjoyable time, dearest," Ingrid said, "but remember not to lose either your head or your heart, for where Fabian is concerned they will both be irretrievable."

"I will remember," Loretta said a little uncertainly.

She did not realise as the door shut behind her that her cousin looked after her with a worried expression on her face.

* * * * * * *

Carrying a velvet wrap over her arm, Loretta went slowly down the stairs, and just as she reached the hall a footman came hurrying from the front door to say:

"A gentleman is waiting for you, *Madame*, and asks if you will hurry, as his horses are a little restless."

Loretta did not stop to think it was somewhat strange that Fabian's horses, with which she had driven already, had always seemed perfectly trained.

She hurried down the steps to where a footman was holding open the door of a closed carriage.

She could only think it even stranger that Fabian should be waiting for her inside.

Then as she climbed in she found that the carriage was empty.

As she realised it, the door was slammed to.

The horses set off, and she was forced to sit down quickly to avoid being thrown onto the floor.

As the carriage drove up the Champs Élysées at what seemed a quite unnecessary speed, she told herself there must be some mistake.

She must attract the attention of the coachman and footman on the box.

There seemed however to be no way of doing so, for the windows were both tightly shut.

She tried to work out in her mind whether this was some strange new idea of the *Marquis*'s to intrigue her, or if, as seemed more likely, there had been some mistake.

It was then a frightening suspicion came into her mind, so frightening that she was afraid to put it into words.

She bent forward and tried again to open the windows, but they were tightly closed and because they were travelling at such a speed she dared not attempt to open the carriage-door.

"What is .. happening? What can .. be happening?" she asked.

Then as she wondered wildly what she should do, if her worst suspicions were confirmed, she realised they were almost at the end of the Boulevard.

The houses were now more widely spaced, and she thought, although she was not sure, that they were on the edge of the Bois.

The horse turned in through some drive-gates and proceeded a little way through a flower-filled garden before they came to a standstill outside the portico of a large house.

"There *is* a mistake," Loretta told herself consolingly. "The coachman must have gone to the wrong house and picked up the wrong person. It is my fault for not being more suspicious and not thinking it strange that the *Marquis* did not come into the house."

The carriage-door was opened by a footman and she said to him in French:

"To whom does this house belong?"

"*Monsieur* is waiting for you, *Madame*, inside," the footman replied.

"And what is the name of *Monsieur*?" Loretta persisted.

"He is waiting, *Madame*, and asks if you will join him."

Because there seemed to be nothing she could do and it was impossible to go on arguing, Loretta stepped out of the carriage, saying as she did so:

"Tell the coachman to wait. There has been some mistake, and I must explain to your Master that I must go back to where I came from."

As she spoke she walked into the hall where another servant moved ahead of her to lead her up a broad stairway to what she expected would be a Salon on the First Floor.

The house looked well-furnished and very luxurious.

She began to think that what had happened was a genuine mistake and she would find herself with a party of people who had no idea who she was.

'I must insist that I am taken back at once,' Loretta thought, 'otherwise the *Marquis* will arrive and wonder what has happened to me.'

She caught sight of a clock at the top of the stairs and told herself she had been very stupid in the first place to think it was the Marquis.

Last night he had been exactly on time and now it was only just after eight o'clock.

She must have been driving for at least ten minutes since leaving the Champs Élysées.

A servant opened the door and was silent as she passed him into a large room.

She had only taken a few steps when she stopped dead.

Standing waiting for her were not strangers, as she had expected, but one man – the *Comte* Eugene de Marais.

He was looking somewhat strange.

It took Loretta a second or two to realise he was not wearing evening-dress, but a heavily padded brocade coat.

It was like her father sometimes wore after hunting, though a very much more elaborate version.

She looked at him wide-eyed, wondering what she could say and how she could express her horror at being brought to him in such an extraordinary manner.

Then she realised that the room was not a Salon but a bedroom.

There was a large draped divan-like bed against one wall and the *Comte* was standing in front of a long mirror which reflected both his back and the bed.

Softly shaded lights gave the room an air of seduction.

Loretta found her voice.

III

"How dare you .. bring me here like this!" she began.

As she spoke she heard the door shut behind her and the *Comte* moved forward to say:

"You have come! This is what I have been longing for, my beautiful lady, and now there is no question of your not dining with me, as I wish you to do."

"As I told you this morning, *Monsieur*, I have another engagement," Loretta said, "and I am appalled at your extraordinary behaviour."

He had almost reached her and because she was frightened she moved back towards the door and tried to turn the handle.

As she did so she realised that the door was locked.

Then as she looked again at the *Comte* she saw the amusement in his eyes.

"There is no escape, my lovely one!" he said. "You have fought me in a manner I find entrancing since we first sat together at dinner, and if you continue to fight me, I assure you I shall find it exceedingly alluring and very exciting."

"Having got me here by a trick, how can you expect me to do .. anything but .. fight you?" Loretta asked.

"I want you!" the *Comte* said in the deep velvet tones which Loretta found very frightening.

She stared at him.

Then as if she felt that the way she was speaking was perhaps a mistake, she said:

"Please .. be civilised about this. You know I had no wish to come .. here, and I can only .. beg of you as a .. gentleman to .. let me go."

"And how disappointed you would be if I did!" the *Comte* replied. "However, as you said, we will be civilised about it, and the first thing is to have a glass of champagne. There is no hurry, for we have the whole night ahead of us."

The way he spoke made Loretta feel that she might

scream at him with horror.

Then with a pride and self-control she did not know she possessed she managed to say:

"I would like a glass of champagne. But you can imagine, I am deeply perturbed at being .. abducted in this .. extraordinary way."

"I told you that I always get my own way," the *Comte* replied. "Now, come and sit down. I want to look at you and to assure you, in case you doubt my word, that I have never seen anybody more beautiful, nor so utterly and completely desirable."

He gestured to Loretta to follow him as he moved to a sofa that had its back to the heavily curtained bow-window. In front of it was a table.

On it she saw there was a bottle of champagne in a huge gold ice-cooler on a gold tray, and a number of decanters and bottles.

She sat down, feeling that if she did not keep a tight hold on herself, she would run to the door, banging on it with her fists and screaming to be let out.

She was sure that if she did so the *Comte*'s servants would pay no attention.

It was horrifying to be aware that a servant had locked her in as he must have been instructed to do.

The *Comte* sat down beside her and she saw that beneath his open velvet coat he was wearing his evening-trousers and a thin lawn shirt.

But instead of the conventional stiff collar there was a soft satin tie around his neck which she realised would be much easier to remove.

She felt faint at the idea, and tried not to look at the bed they were facing, having already seen that it had silk sheets edged with lace and fat satin pillows engraved with the *Comte*'s monogram.

He poured some champagne into two glasses saying as he did so:

"A golden wine which echoes the gold in your hair, and I suggest you have one of these sandwiches which are made with a pâté I have sent from Strasbourg, or, if you prefer, there is caviar."

Because she was afraid she might faint, Loretta took a sip of the champagne and the *Comte* said:

"Later we will have supper in the next room, but first, my beautiful lady, I intend to teach you, as no Englishman could do, the passions of love, the secrets of which were known to the Ancient Egyptians and to the Indians, many of whom were famous lovers."

The way he spoke made her feel as if every word he uttered was a delight to him, and as if in some unpleasant way it excited him.

She felt too that he looked at her as if he mentally undressed her.

Because she could not help it, she shrank away from him.

He laughed softly.

"In a little while," he said, "I will make you mine. Then, my adorable, unawakened Englishwoman, you will become more mature, more feminine, and, although it seems impossible, even more desirable than you are at this moment."

Now, before Loretta could move, he put his arm around her and taking her glass from her hand, drew her closer to him.

She tried to resist him, but realised he was exceedingly strong.

"No, no!" she cried.

But he merely pulled her relentlessly and now her body was touching his.

"Fabian help me .. help me," she prayed.

It was then, as she sent out a cry for help in her heart, that she knew what to do.

She put out her hand as if in protest.

As she did so she knocked the earring which Ingrid had lent her, and which was only clipped to her ear, onto the floor.

She gave a cry of consternation:

"My earring!" she cried. "Do not stand on it, it is very fragile!"

The *Comte* looked down to where the earring was lying just beneath a low table.

As he bent down Loretta leant over him.

Picking up an unopened bottle of mineral water that was standing on the gold tray beside the decanter, she brought it down with all her force on the back of his head.

He fell forward with a groan and as he did so she hit him again.

Then rising to give more force to the blow she struck him for the third time.

As he collapsed onto the floor between the table and the sofa, she heard a noise behind her.

Turning her head involuntarily, she saw the curtains part and Fabian came into the room.

She gave out a cry of relief which seemed to echo round the walls.

Throwing the bottle down on the sofa she ran round it to fling herself against him saying as she did so:

"I have . . killed him! I have . . killed him! Oh, Fabian . . I have killed . . him!"

# CHAPTER SIX

Fabian put his arms around Loretta and held her close against him.

Then as she hid her face against his shoulder she murmured in a voice he could hardly hear:

"I . . I have . . k . . killed him! W . . will I be taken to . . p . . prison and be . . guillotined?"

He felt her whole body tremble at the thought and said quietly and calmly:

"It is all right, my darling, leave everything to me."

As he spoke he drew her through the curtains and an open window onto the balcony.

Because she was still clinging to him desperately he very gently moved her to the support of the stone balustrade and said:

"Stand here and breathe deeply. I am going back to see exactly what has happened."

"H . . he is . . d . . dead!"

Obeying almost like a child what Fabian had told her to do, she clung onto the balustrade, feeling the cold of it was somehow helpful and she could lean against it.

He disappeared through the window.

Loretta shut her eyes, feeling that what had happened could not be true, but must be part of some terrible nightmare.

But she knew, with a throbbing of her heart and a dryness of her lips, and a feeling of terror that was still inside her, what the *Comte* had meant to do.

She had only saved herself by a miracle.

It seemed to her a long time that she stood there, feeling as if she might collapse on the balcony.

She was afraid, however, that if she did so, Fabian would despise her.

"I must control myself and be brave," she tried to say.

But she knew she felt weak and helpless, while waves of nausea seemed to be rising in her.

Then when she felt she could not bear it any longer and she must go inside and see what was happening, Fabian returned.

She heard his footsteps behind her and turned to fling herself against him.

He held her very close and the strength of his arms was an unbelievable comfort.

"It is all right, my precious," he said. "He is not dead!"

"N .. not .. dead?"

It was almost impossible for her to say the words.

"No, he is alive, but you have been very rough with him, and he will suffer the effects of concussion for some time, which he richly deserves!"

Fabian's voice was harsh, but all Loretta could think of was that she was safe.

She would not be imprisoned or guillotined, since the *Comte* was not dead, as she had thought he must be.

Fabian drew her a little closer and she thought his lips were on her hair as he said:

"Now I want you to be very brave, for as I cannot ask you to climb down the way I climbed up, we will have to walk to the front door, where my carriage will be waiting."

"B .. but we .. cannot get out ..." Loretta faltered,

"the . . the door is . . l . . locked."

"I am aware of that," Fabian said harshly, "but fortunately there is another door from the room where you were to dine."

She looked up at him enquiringly.

As he saw her face was very pale, her eyes still dark with fear, her lips trembling, he said gently as if he was speaking to a child:

"Just be brave for a little while longer. We must not let the servants think there is any reason why you should be overwhelmingly upset by what has occurred."

What he said made her stiffen and raise her chin.

There was a very tender expression in his eyes as he looked at her for a long moment.

Then he put his arm round her shoulders and steered her through the door behind them.

He parted the curtains, and for a moment Loretta dared not look at the battered man she had left lying on the floor.

Then she saw that Fabian must have lifted the *Comte* onto the bed.

He was lying there against the satin pillows with his eyes closed.

His padded coat and his shirt were open as if Fabian had felt his heart.

When she would have asked the question, Fabian picked up her velvet wrap, and slipped her arm through his.

He drew her firmly to a door beside the fireplace in the bedroom, which led into a *Boudoir* where there stood a table laid for two.

The lights were very low and seductive.

But Fabian propelled Loretta towards the door which opened when he turned the handle.

Without speaking he escorted her along the corridor and down the stairs up which she had followed the servant when she first arrived.

There were several flunkeys and an elderly man who appeared to be in charge in the hall.

Loretta was sure they would be looking in astonishment at Fabian.

They were wondering how she could have suddenly materialised from the locked bedroom of their Master.

Fabian helped Loretta down the last step of the stairs before he said with a note of authority in his voice:

"Your Master is unwell! Attend to him and send for a doctor immediately."

When he had finished speaking he did not wait to hear any reply, but went with Loretta out through the front door and down the steps to where his carriage was waiting.

He helped her into it and sat beside her, and as soon as the footman had shut the door the horses drove off.

It was then that the self-control which Loretta summoned up in order to obey his instructions broke, and she burst into tears.

It was as if she was swept away by a tempest of her own fears.

She could no more control her tears than stop the Seine from flowing.

She cried as a child might have done, the tears running from her eyes to wet Fabian's evening-cloak.

She was blind and deaf to everything except her own misery.

He held her very close and when her tears abated a little he said:

"It is all right, my precious, innocent little goddess. You were quite safe, from the moment I saw his carriage driving away and was told you had already left I realised what had happened."

"You .. knew he would bring me to his .. house?" Loretta managed to whisper.

"I know his methods only too well!" Fabian answered angrily.

"Although you nearly killed him, my darling, it was no less than I intended to do myself if he had hurt you in any way."

"I . . I was . . frightened . . very frightened!"

"Of course you were, but you must have known that I would save you."

"I was . . praying that you would," Loretta said, "and crying out to you in my . . h . . heart."

"I heard you," Fabian answered. "Fortunately I have been in the *Comte*'s house before, and guessed where the swine would have taken you. So I climbed up onto the balcony. It is a fairly easy climb as there is a trellis-work beneath it. But if I had had to storm the Bastille, I would still have come to you."

Loretta tried to smile, but it was too difficult.

She did indeed manage to stop crying, but she still hid her face against Fabian's shoulder.

Then she gave a little cry.

"I left my . . earring behind. It is Ingrid's! If anybody finds it they might know I was . . there!"

Fabian opened his hand and she saw that the diamond and pearl earring lay in his palm.

"You . . found it!"

"I heard you say as I stepped onto the balcony: 'I have dropped my earring!'"

"Thank you . . oh, thank . . you!" Loretta said.

Then for no particular reason except that it was all so overwhelming, the tears were running down her cheeks again.

Fabian wiped them away very tenderly, until as the horses came to a standstill Loretta said:

"I . . I cannot let anyone . . see me like this!"

"No, of course not," he replied. "That is why I have brought you to my house."

Loretta looked at him and he said gently:

"It will be quite proper for you to come here because

my grandmother, the *Duchesse de* Mellerio, is staying with me at the moment. She is very old and has her dinner in bed."

At that moment a footman opened the door, and Fabian alighted and helped Loretta from the carriage.

She bent her head so that the servants, and there seemed to be quite a number of them, would not see her face.

Fabian led her across what she thought was a large hall into a room on the other side of it.

As she did so he said to the servant who opened the door:

"Tell the Chef I require a light dinner for two with dishes that he can prepare quickly. And bring me a bottle of champagne."

He drew Loretta into a room which she felt must be one of which was particularly his own.

There were exquisite pieces of French furniture around the walls, and a very comfortable-looking sofa and chairs.

Despite the fact that everything about it was exquisitely French, it was also a man's room and there was an atmosphere of masculinity which was unmistakable.

Fabian helped Loretta onto the sofa, then put his soft linen handkerchief into her hand.

She wiped away the tear stains from her cheeks, but when she looked up at him her long eye-lashes were still wet.

Although she was not aware of it, she looked very pale, and without the cosmetics which had been washed away by her tears, very pathetic.

Fabian did not speak until a footman came into the room with a bottle of champagne in an ice-bucket and two glasses.

He filled one and set it down on a small table beside Loretta and handed another to his Master.

Then he put the ice-bucket down on the table on the other side of the fireplace and left the room.

"Drink a little," Fabian said gently, "it is what you need."

Because she was too weak not to obey him she did as she was told.

Then as she wiped her face again with Fabian's handkerchief he said:

"You look very lovely, but desperately in need of protection. This sort of thing must never happen to you again, and that is why my darling, I have something to ask you."

"What is .. it?"

She thought it strange that for a moment he seemed to be feeling for words. Then he said:

"I love you, and I know, although you will not admit it, that you love me. We are complete and one person, so we have to be together. That is why I am asking you, my darling, to come away with me."

For a moment Loretta did not understand, then as her eyes searched his, he said:

"For a little while, until your husband divorces you, we shall be like your friend Ingrid and Hugh Galston, but I think our love is big enough for neither of us to mind being ostracised by the Social World. In fact, I think that World will not be of the least interest to either of us, now or in the future."

"I do not .. know what .. you are saying .. I do not understand," Loretta faltered.

"I think you do," Fabian contradicted. "You are intelligent enough to know that love is irresistible, and when we find real love, the love we all seek, it is impossible to deny it."

He paused for a moment, and taking her hand turned it over in his as he said:

"Such a very little hand, and yet, my precious, you

hold my heart and my whole happiness in it. If you refuse me, I shall never be a whole man again."

Loretta shut her eyes for a moment; then she said in a very low voice:

"How could you .. of all people .. with your background, your .. possessions, and with your position in France do .. anything that would .. cause such a .. scandal?"

Fabian laughed, and it was a very happy sound.

"Scandal? What scandal?" he asked. "The chattering of people who are merely envious because they do not feel what we feel! Moreover, my darling, we shall not be here to listen to all the nonsense they will say about us."

Loretta made a little murmur, but she did not interrupt and he went on:

"I am going to take you away, first to North Africa, where I own a lot of land, and which I think you will find as fascinating as I do. Later we can live in Normandy where I have an estate which belonged to my mother. It is so different in every way from my father's *Château* on the Loire, that we might as well be in another world."

He paused and his fingers tightened on hers as he said:

"If you are not happy in France, the world is a large place, and I know wherever I am with you, we shall be in the 'Utopia' I have always sought."

He smiled as he said:

"It is the Paradise that has always escaped me until, when you came into the Salon the first day of your arrival, I knew that I had found you, and nothing else was of any consequence."

"You .. cannot mean what .. you are .. saying," Loretta murmured.

Then as Fabian looked into her eyes she knew that he was speaking from his heart.

Every word he had said to her was utterly sincere.

"I know what you are thinking," he said softly, "but I

123

also know that, just as you love me, my precious little goddess, explanations between us are quite unnecessary."

His voice deepened.

"I will take you away, I will protect you and love you for the rest of our lives. When we die there will be other lives because it is impossible now for us ever to lose each other again."

Because she was unable to speak she could only look at him.

She was not aware that her eyes seemed to fill her whole face.

Then as the door opened Fabian released her hand and said in a very different voice which seemed irrepressibly gay and happy:

"Now I am going to give you something to eat, then I will take you home. You have been through enough for one night, and tomorrow we will make plans."

Incredible though it seemed afterwards, they sat down at the table and as the servants brought in course after course, each more delicious than the last, Fabian talked.

He made himself so amusing and so fascinating that it was possible for Loretta to forget what had happened, even to laugh at what he said.

It was like, she thought, being part of the iridescence of the fountain in the Bois, as she was swept away by his *Joie de vivre*.

She could no longer be miserable or frightened, only happy because they were together and for the moment nothing else seemed of any consequence.

It was only when their dinner was finished and the servants had cleared the table that Loretta moved to stand looking down into the fireplace, which, because there was no fire, was filled with flowers.

She did not realise that Fabian stood behind her and she started as he asked:

"What is worrying you?"

He did not wait for her to answer but said:

"I will do all the worrying in the future, and I want you to smile and look happy as you were doing just now. Leave everything to me, my precious."

"B . . but . . I cannot do . . that."

"Why not? That is what I am here for – to look after you."

"I know . . but . . .'

"There are no 'buts'," Fabian interrupted. "You are mine, Lora, and as I really will kill any man who frightens you again, you just have to leave everything in my hands."

"I . . I cannot do that . . you do not . . understand," Loretta said.

She was thinking that perhaps she should tell him who she was and explain what had happened.

Then before she could formulate her words or decide what she wished to do, Fabian put his fingers under her chin and turned her face up to his.

"You are so lovely, so unbelievably lovely," he said, "but so much more than that."

His voice was very deep and solemn.

Yet because he was touching her Loretta felt little shafts of sunshine, as she had before, running through her.

"I adore your beauty, and I want and desire you! How could I do anything else?" he asked in a low voice almost as if he was speaking to himself. "But I also worhip your aura of purity. I know you are good, and I have known very few good women in my life."

Loretta's eyes dropped for a moment before his, but he did not release her chin, and he went on:

"But that is not all. I am absolutely sure you are the other half of me – the completion which makes us together one person. As I have already said, I have found you after searching for so long and I will never lose you again!"

He spoke with a determination in his voice which made

Loretta feel he would sweep away any obstacles in his path and fight unceasingly to gain what he desired.

"I love you! I love you, and together we are, even if people do not realise it at first, the perfection of love."

Then his arms were round her, and before she could realise what he was about to do, his lips were on hers.

She knew as her body melted against his that this was what she had wanted.

This was what she had been longing for, although she dared not admit it.

He kissed her until she felt as if they were swept out of the room in which they were standing, and up into the sky.

Now the sunlight in her body became iridescent rainbows that carried her higher and higher until she thought Fabian gave her the stars.

They glittered in her breast and on her lips.

Then they became little tongues of fire answering the fire that she knew was burning in him.

Yet he had himself completely under control. Only when Loretta felt as if she could not experience such ecstatic sensations as he evoked in her and not die from the wonder of them, he raised his head and said in a voice that was curiously unsteady:

"Now do you understand?"

"I . . love you!" Loretta whispered because she could not help herself.

"That is all that matters!" he said quietly.

He had so bewildered her that, before she could realise what was happening, he had put her velvet wrap round her shoulders and had drawn her from the Salon and into the hall.

As they moved towards the door she saw that his carriage was waiting for them.

When the horses drove off, he put his arms round her and held her close against him but he did not kiss her again.

Instead she saw he was looking ahead into their future.

He was seeing it so clearly that it was almost as if he was reading it out to her from pages on which he had written it down.

It was only a short distance from the Marquess's house to the Champs Élysées.

When they arrived Loretta said hurriedly and again a little incoherently:

"I must .. talk to you .. I must explain . . ."

"There is nothing to talk about tonight," Fabian replied. "Tomorrow I will listen to whatever you have to say if it is of real importance. Otherwise, my precious, we are both of us past words."

He kissed her hand, then he said:

"Because I have to look after you and prevent you from being tired after what has been a very emotional upset, I want you to go straight to bed, and remember only what you felt just now when I kissed you."

His lips touched her hand again, then he helped her out of the carriage.

Before she could realise what he was doing, he had taken her into the hall and left her there.

She wanted to cry out to him, to stop him.

But she heard the carriage driving away and knew it was too late and she should have told him that she was not who she pretended to be.

Then as everything seemed to be turning over and over in her mind the Butler said:

"Madame is alone in the Silver Salon."

'I must see Ingrid,' Loretta thought.

The servant went ahead and opened the door of the Silver Salon.

She saw Ingrid looking very beautiful and sitting in one of the blue brocade and gold chairs.

She looked up as Loretta came into the room and exclaimed:

"My dearest, you are back early! I have been so worried as to what had happened to you. I heard you were driven away in a strange carriage before Fabian had come to collect you as arranged."

Loretta drew in her breath, then as she was about to tell Ingrid what had happened, the Marquess came into the room.

Instantly Ingrid's attention was directed towards him.

"Is it all right, Hugh?" she asked, and her voice was anxious. "What did that man want to see you about?"

The Marquess walked in silence until he stood in front of Ingrid.

Then he looked down at her with an expression in his eyes which Loretta thought was very moving as he said:

"My wife died three days ago! And now, my darling, I can ask you to marry me."

Ingrid gave a cry of happiness that brought the tears to Loretta's eyes.

Then as the Marquess put his arms around her Loretta knew that for the moment they would wish to be alone.

Without either of them realising it she slipped out of the room and went up the stairs.

Only when she reached her bedroom did she know what she had to do, and that was to go home.

In the first place Ingrid and Hugh would want to be alone after all they had been through.

This was the opening of a new chapter in their lives and no one outside should intrude on them.

Secondly, quite apart from Ingrid, Loretta knew that she herself had made a decision regarding her future.

She rang the bell for Marie and when she came told her to pack all her clothes as they would be leaving first thing in the morning.

"So soon, *Milady*?" Marie moaned. "I verry happy in Paris. I no wish go back to England."

Loretta was about to say that perhaps it would not be for long.

Then she was afraid in case it was unlucky to anticipate what was not yet decided.

Now she tortured herself with the thought when Fabian knew she had deceived him he would be angry.

Perhaps too because he was unconventional and different in so many ways he would not agree to marry the girl his father had chosen for him.

He would prefer the dangerous and wild adventure of running away with a married woman and defying the Social World.

There were a million questions that Loretta was to ask herself.

Not only during the night when she could not sleep, but also the next morning when she and Marie drove to the Gare du Nord before Ingrid had been called.

During the night she had written two letters.

The first one to Ingrid, thanking her for being so kind and understanding.

She told her how thrilled and delighted she was that she could now marry the man she loved.

She ended her letter:

*"You will not understand, but one day I may be able to explain to you that I want to marry the man I love. It will not be wrong, as you thought it might be, but right, completely and absolutely right for us both.*

*Just as you and Hugh have the love that conquers all things, and before which everything else pales into insignificance, I have found the same .. but please do NOT tell Fabian who I am. There are still many difficulties and obstacles."*

To Fabian she wrote:

*"I love you .. I love you with all my heart .. but
perhaps when you know how I have deceived you, you
will no longer love me, and it will be my own fault for
doing anything so outrageous as to come alone to
Paris.*

*I was searching, as you were, for someone of whom
I had dreamt, someone I thought I would never find.
So perhaps you will forgive me.*

*Lora."*

She wondered what he would think when he read it. She
wondered if because obviously he would guess she had
gone home to England, he would think it worth his while
to follow her.

Perhaps he would return to the life he was living before
she arrived, and particularly to *Madame* Julie St. Gervaise.

'There have been so many women in his life, and I am
just a falling star who held his attention for a minute, but
whom he will find it easy to forget,' Loretta thought.

Then as the train carried her towards Calais she wanted
to cry out because of the agony consuming her at losing
Fabian.

Her love that enveloped her to the point where it was
impossible to think or feel anything but love.

"I love him! I love him!" she told herself over and over
again.

The wheels beneath her seemed to be repeating the
same words:

"I love him! I love him!"

Marie, who had been sulking because of their sudden
return to England, suddenly leant across to ask in a
worried voice:

"You all right, *Milady*? You verry pale. Perhaps you
starting bad cold?"

"No, I am all right, Marie," Loretta managed to say.

But she knew that was untrue.

She would never be all right again until Fabian was with her, protecting her, keeping her safe, and loving her.

A million times she asked herself whether she had done the wrong thing in coming away without seeing him first.

If it had not been for the death of Hugh's wife and her knowledge that she should not intrude on their happiness, she might have confessed to Fabian the truth when he called for her in the morning, as he had said he would do.

But she had been desperately afraid of seeing the disillusionment in his eyes.

She could hear Ingrid saying so positively when she first arrived:

"Fabian will take no notice of you if he thinks you are a *jeune fille*."

She had gone on to say that she was sure he had never talked to one, unless she was a relative.

How then, after she had met him under false pretences, would he react to the truth.

She was not only a *jeune fille*, but the one chosen for him by his father?

She knew without being told that, while Fabian was fond of his father, he also resented the *Duc* treating him as if he was still under his authority.

'He is so much a man, so much an individual in his own right,' Loretta thought. 'Of course he wants to be his own master and decide everything for himself!'

The more she thought about it, the more she could see her happiness slipping away and a gulf spreading between her and Fabian.

The distance between them lengthened and lengthened as the train drew her towards Calais.

. . . . . . .

She and Marie caught the midday Steamer to Dover.

Finally there was a long and tiresome wait at the

junction for the train that would carry them back to their local station.

Loretta had sent a telegram from Dover for a carriage to meet her, and she was indeed thankful that it was there.

But she really found it difficult to think of anything but Fabian.

Fabian telling her of his love, Fabian holding her in his arms, Fabian finding her at the *Comte*'s house when he had climbed up to the balcony to save her!

Fabian! Fabian!

She knew if she never saw him again he would haunt her for the rest of her life and she would die with his name on her lips.

Then she was at home in her own bed, tired out by the journey, only thankful it was too late to see Cousin Emily.

She felt she had been away for a hundred years and had lived a different life on another Planet.

Still there was only Fabian.

Her last thought before finally she fell asleep was that his lips were on hers.

Once again the stars were glittering in her breasts and their glitter had become little tongues of fire.

. . . . . . .

When she awoke in the morning, she felt she had dreamed everything and none of it could be true.

She made no effort to get up as she usually did to go riding.

For the moment she was not interested even in the horses.

It merely passed through her mind that if she sent a message to Christopher by Ben, he would be waiting for her in the afternoon where they always met.

Then for the first time since she had come home, she felt the tears gathering in her eyes.

She knew that like every other woman who had loved Fabian, she too was crying for him.

She had held him for one, brief, marvellous moment and he had told her of his love.

Now she had thrown it away, or rather in becoming herself she had lost him.

In doing so, she had lost everything in life that was worth having, everything she wanted now or for the future.

Finally, when it was quite late in the morning, she rose and went downstairs.

"Your Ladyship's not riding?" Sarah asked as she helped her dress.

"No, not today," Loretta replied.

Instead she sent to the stables for the cart in which she often drove herself around the estate.

Taking Ben with her, she drove into the village to see Marie.

Simply because Marie had been with her in France and therefore formed a kind of link with Fabian, she was the only person she wanted to see at the moment, and to talk to.

Marie was delighted to see her.

"*Bonjour, Milady!*" she said. "I glad you come. I sad, verry sad, to be back in England. I miss *ma belle France.*"

"I miss it too," Loretta said, and knew she was referring to one man.

Marie made her coffee, then she said in a tone she sometimes used when she felt emotional:

"You not worry, *ma petite*. You marry the *Marquis*! You both verry 'appy!"

"Oh, Marie!" Loretta cried. "Perhaps now when he realises I have deceived him he will refuse to marry me."

Marie laughed.

"That not true! *Monsieur le Marquis* in love – servant tell me he love you as he never love any other lady!"

"Why should he say that?" Loretta asked. "And how would he know anyway?"

Marie laughed again.

"The French understand *l'amour*. The coachman of *Monsieur le Marquis* tell me he never know his Master feel for any lady what he feel for you."

"But how could he know?" Loretta wanted to ask logically.

Yet somehow, despite herself, she was cheered up by what Marie had said.

She drove back home feeling a little happier than she had before she went to the village.

She had luncheon alone.

Then she walked into the garden, moving restlessly across the green lawn towards the yew hedges which enclosed the Rose Garden.

In the centre of it was a small fountain, very unlike the large one in the Bois.

Yet as its water was thrown a few feet up into the air and the sunshine made iridescent rainbows of it, they seemed to be moving within her as they had when Fabian had kissed her.

"I shall never feel like that over any man again," she told herself.

Then it was an unbearable agony to know that he was so far away not only in miles, but in the way they had vibrated to each other.

They had seemed, she thought, to be one person.

Now he might have deliberately turned away from her, not only physically but mentally and spiritually – above all in his heart.

"Oh, Fabian! Fabian!" she cried.

She heard her voice ring out in the quietness of the garden.

She felt as if the water from the fountain carried it like a prayer up into the sky.

Then as she turned away, half-blinded by the tears in her eyes, she saw him coming through the roses towards her.

# CHAPTER SEVEN

Loretta felt her heart beating wildly.

At the same time an irrepressible joy swept through her body, making her feel as if she came alive because he was there.

He moved slowly towards her and only when he stopped a few feet from her did he say in a strange voice:

"Am I to understand that Lady Brompton is in fact Lady Loretta Court?"

"You .. did not .. know?"

"I had not the slightest idea!"

Loretta looked at him in bewilderment.

"Then .. how is it that .. you are .. here? How did you .. find me?"

She was aware as she spoke that the expression on Fabian's face was grim, and he was staring at her as if he could not believe she was real.

After a moment he answered:

"When you ran away in that extraordinary and cruel manner without saying good-bye to me, I thought I should go mad!"

"Did Ingrid tell you .. who I was?"

"No. She lied, most convincingly."

"Then how . . ."

"Hugh Galston was more obliging. He told me he thought a girl called Lady Loretta Court could help me."

"So you came .. here."

"To ask her if she knew where I could find Lady Brompton."

There was a frightening pause before he asked:

"How could you deceive me and then run away?"

"You are .. angry with .. me?"

"Very angry!" he said. "I thought you trusted me and I also believed that you loved me."

"I do love .. you," Loretta replied in a very low voice. "I love you .. but I felt I could not .. tell you who I .. was."

"Why not?"

"Because I had .. come to Paris to .. find out about you."

"Find out about me?" he interrupted. "Why? For what reason?"

Loretta stared at him. Then as he was obviously waiting for an answer she said:

"I .. I thought .. it was impossible for me to .. marry a man I did .. not love."

There was a silence in which Fabian was very still. Then he said:

"What has your marriage to do with it? I may be dense, but I find what you are saying quite incomprehensible."

Loretta looked up at him and thought she must be imagining this conversation because it was so strange.

So different from what she had expected if she ever saw Fabian again.

Then looking away from him because she felt desperately shy, she said:

"I .. I came to Paris because .. Papa told me I had to marry you and he had .. arranged it with your father."

"Is that the truth?"

Fabian spoke loudly, then he reached out and took hold

of Loretta by the shoulders and turned her around to face him.

"Is what you are saying true?" he asked furiously. "That your father and mine plotted our marriage?"

Because he was touching her, Loretta felt a thrill run through her body, even though she was afraid of his anger.

"They .. they arranged it at a .. race-meeting," she said. "Surely your father .. must have .. told you!"

"He told me nothing! He has been ordering me, pleading with me, begging me for years to marry again, but I had no intention whatever of obeying him!"

The way he spoke made Loretta feel that she had indeed lost him completely and the world seemed to have gone dark.

Then as if he forced himself to be more controlled he said harshly:

"I think you had better explain to me from the beginning what all this means. I am in fact utterly bewildered."

He released her as he spoke and Loretta, trembling, indicated a wooden seat under some trees at the other side of the garden.

It was impossible to speak because she felt as if her voice had died in her throat.

Instead she walked towards the seat, knowing that Fabian was following her.

She saw unhappily that he sat down as far away from her as possible.

Then he turned a little towards her to say in the same hard tone of voice he had used before:

"I suggest you start from the beginning and tell me what all this is about."

"H .. how could I have thought .. how could I have imagined .. that you did not .. know?"

Fabian did not reply and after a moment she said in a low, unhappy tone which was very unlike the way she usually spoke:

"Papa returned from the races last week to .. tell me his horse had .. beaten the .. *Duc de* Sauerdun's."

She thought Fabian might make some comment, but he did not speak.

When she glanced at him again his lips were set tightly in a hard line.

"Papa was exuberant, not only because he had won the race," she went on, "but because the *Duc* had .. suggested that I should .. marry his .. son."

"And you agreed?"

"I .. I tried to tell Papa it was absolutely impossible for me to marry a man I had never seen .. and whom I did not love."

"And what was his reply?"

"He flew into one of his rages, and said that if he had to drag me to the altar I would marry the *Marquis de* Sauerdun .. because it was a good match .. and one of which .. he approved."

Again she looked at Fabian, and saw that now he was staring across the garden.

She went on miserably, knowing that he was very angry:

"I knew it was no use .. arguing or pleading with Papa .. and I suddenly had the idea that the only way I could .. convince him that I could not .. marry you was .. to go to Paris and .. find out what you were like .. without your knowing who .. I was."

"So you knew there was something to find out?"

"I thought there must be .. because everything was to be .. done in such a hurry .. You were to stay with us during Royal Ascot week .. and then our engagement was to be .. announced at the Ball Papa would give .. here when the race-meeting was over."

She knew without even looking at him that this made Fabian angrier than ever.

She could feel his vibrations, and she told herself she was talking away her happiness.

She was killing everything that mattered to her life.

"I .. remembered," she continued after a moment, "that my Cousin Ingrid, of whom we were never .. allowed even to speak, was living in Paris, and I found out her address from an old maid living in the village who had once worked for us and who is French."

"And you came to France alone?"

"Marie came with me, and it was far easier than I expected. When I told Ingrid why I had .. come she .. understood."

"What did she understand?"

Loretta paused until Fabian repeated:

"What did she understand?"

"That you were .. not the right sort of husband for me .. and you would make me .. very unhappy."

"Did she say anything else?"

"She told me that she thought she .. knew why the *Duc*, your father .. was in such a .. hurry to get you .. married."

"And what was the reason?"

Reluctantly, as if the words were dragged from her, Loretta answered:

"Ingrid .. said you were .. infatuated .. with a widow .. whom it would be .. possible .. because she was well-bred .. for you to marry .. if you wished to .. do so."

"I can follow my father's thoughts on the subject," Fabian said sarcastically.

Loretta gave a deep sigh and realised as she looked down at her hands that they were shaking.

"So you and Ingrid," Fabian went on, "decided to deceive me by dressing you up as Lady Brompton!"

"It was because I insisted on .. meeting you without your knowing who I was .. and Ingrid said you would

140

certainly avoid having anything to do with a *jeune fille* ..
in fact she doubted if you had ever .. spoken to one."

For the first time there was just a slight twist of a smile
at the corners of Fabian's mouth.

"And you thought your disguise was effective," he said,
"and that I was deceived into believing you were a sophisticated married woman."

"You asked me to luncheon and to dine with you."

"Then what happened?"

There was silence and Fabian repeated insistently:

"What happened, Lora?"

"I .. I fell in .. love with you," Loretta replied in a
voice he could hardly hear, "like all the other .. silly
women to whom you have ever .. paid any .. attention."

"You fell in love?" he asked quietly. "And yet you ran
away without explaining, without telling me the truth."

"I .. I knew that Ingrid and the Marquess wanted to
be alone, and also .. because you were so very .. different
from what I expected .. I could not bear to tell you ..
knowing that you would be .. angry with me."

"I was different from what you expected? In what
way?"

Loretta made a helpless little gesture with her hand.

"You know exactly what I .. mean," she said. "You
talked to me as no one has ever .. talked to me before ..
and I could not help .. loving you."

She gave a little sob on the last words and felt the tears
come into her eyes.

Then almost as if she must justify herself she said
again:

"How could I have .. imagined for one moment that
you did not .. know what your father was .. planning?"

"I can see how cleverly he had thought it all out,"
Fabian said slowly. "He had asked me to come with him
to Ascot this year as a special favour, and because I always
enjoy being in England, I agreed."

He paused for a moment as if he was working it out.

"He would then have insisted that I came to stay here at your father's house and before I could have any say in the matter our engagement would have been announced."

"That is . . exactly what they . . planned," Loretta said, "and why I knew I had to circumvent it, since I could not . . marry you."

"Why were you so certain?"

Loretta drew in her breath, then she told the truth.

"I had always dreamed that . . one day I would . . find a man whom I would love . . and who would . . love me . . ."

"And when you met me?"

"You *were* . . the man of who I had dreamt! I knew it as soon as I felt your . . vibrations, and I was quite . . certain after we had talked . . together."

There was a long silence, while Loretta felt as if Fabian was miles away from her, disappearing over a distant horizon, and she would never see him again.

Because she knew that to plead with him to go on loving her would be to behave like every other woman he had loved, she told herself she must have some pride.

If he never thought of her again, at least he would know she had courage.

With an almost superhuman effort she rose from the seat on which she had been sitting and said:

"Now you know the truth . . I understand exactly what . . you are feeling . . and I think it would be . . wise if you left . . immediately as there is no . . point in our going on . . talking about it."

Fabian did not move, but merely looked at her to ask:

"Is that what you want?"

Loretta shut her eyes.

She knew she was crucifying herself, but she would not, as she longed to do, throw herself at his feet and beg him to stay.

"I am .. thinking of you," she said. "If it is known that you have been here .. which at the moment is unlikely .. unless you told the servants who you were .. it will eventually reach my father's ears when he returns .. and things might be .. even more difficult than they are .. already."

"So you intend to tell him that we are not to be married?"

"I will be able to .. do so if you do .. not come to stay as arranged for Ascot."

Fabian rose slowly to his feet.

"So you think I should return to Paris and forget about my pursuit of Lady Brompton?"

"That should be .. easy, as she does not .. exist."

"And you? Will you forget what you felt when I kissed you?" he asked. "What we both felt by the cascade in the Bois . . .?"

He would have gone on, but Loretta could not bear it. She put up her hands as if she was pushing away from him as she said:

"Stop! You are only making .. things more .. difficult. Please .. please .. go away .. at once!"

As she spoke she realised he was standing very close behind her.

Once again he put his hands on her shoulders to turn her around.

Now it was not a rough gesture, but a gentle one.

"And if I go," he asked, "are you prepared to come with me?"

She looked up at him, her eyes very wide, not understanding. At the same time she knew instinctively that he was no longer angry.

Fabian smiled and it transformed his face.

"You are so lovely," he said, "so ridiculously, incredibly beautiful! How could I lose you?"

For a moment Loretta felt she could not have heard him aright.

Yet the rapture that coursed through her whole body was like forked lightning.

Her eyes seemed to have caught the iridescence of the rainbows in the fountain as she said, because she was afraid she was mistaken:

"What .. are you saying? What are you .. asking me to do?"

"I have a wonderful idea, my darling," Fabian said, "but I am afraid you may not agree to it."

"Agree to .. what?"

It was difficult to understand what he was saying when her heart was singing so loudly.

All she was conscious of was the expression in his eyes which she dared not believe was one of love.

"Do you really think I could lose you now?" he asked. "If nothing else, it would be very interesting to get to know a *'jeune fille'*!"

"Then you are .. not angry with .. me?"

"Not any more!"

"You still .. love me .. a little?"

In answer his arms went around her and he drew her closer to him.

Then while her lips were trembling and ready for his he looked down at her for a long moment before he said:

"I love you! I adore you! I worship you! Is that enough?"

"Oh .. Fabian .. !"

The tears that had been at the back of her eyes all the time she was explaining to him what had happened, overflowed and ran down her cheeks.

Then as his lips were on hers, holding her captive, she felt as if the Heavens had opened and a Divine Light encircled them both.

Fabian kissed her possessively, passionately, demandingly.

The garden whirled around them and they were no longer human, but one with the Gods.

When at last he raised his head Loretta whispered:

"I love you . . I love you . . Oh . . Fabian . . I love you . . and when I thought I had . . lost you . . I wanted to die!"

"You will not die, my precious little goddess," he said, "but live with me, happily and for ever."

Then he said in a different tone:

"You still have not answered my question."

"Which . . one?"

"I asked you if you would come away with me."

She looked at him a little puzzled and he said:

"Because I cannot bear to be manipulated, because it would somehow be humiliating for us both to let our fathers think they have arranged everything, whether we want it or not, I suggest we elope!"

"Elope?"

Loretta could hardly say the word.

Fabian laughed, and it was a very happy sound.

"It was what I asked you to do before, and because I knew you loved me as I love you, I thought it was unlikely you would refuse."

His eyes twinkled as he went on:

"Despite that mysterious husband who had apparently not only taught you nothing about love, but had never kissed you."

Loretta gave a little murmur and hid her face against his shoulder.

"Did that . . make you . . suspicious?"

"I was suspicious before that," Fabian replied, "first because no one who was really a married woman could be so obviously innocent, and certainly not exude an aura of purity."

Loretta felt shy as he continued:

"I know this from your vibrations, which I felt so

strongly because they were something I had never en-
countered before."

"You do not think because I am .. me .. I .. will ..
bore you?"

"I am quite certain teaching you about love will be the
most exciting and thrilling thing I have ever done in my
life!"

He kissed her forehead before he went on:

"But I am sure if we have to go through the farce of
pretending we are meeting for the first time when I arrived
here after the races, of announcing our engagement and
then a large, boring, fashionable wedding with all my
relatives saying what a terrible husband I shall be, it will
spoil our happiness."

"Of course it .. will," Loretta agreed. "Oh, Fabian, I
will do .. anything you want .. me to do . . ."

He put his fingers under her chin and turned her face
up to his.

"Do you really mean that?"

He did not kiss her as she expected, but said:

"You are quite sure you will not mind not having a
number of plain bride's-maids trailing enviously behind
you, and a huge, indigestible wedding-cake, and hearing
me make an inane and embarrassing speech?"

The way he spoke was so funny that Loretta laughed.
Then she said:

"I could not .. bear any of it! Take me away, please ..
take me .. away."

"Very well," he agreed, "we will elope and there will
be nothing those scheming fathers of ours can do about
it!"

"They will .. try to .. stop us."

Loretta gave a little shiver as she spoke, knowing how
it would undoubtedly send her father into one of his
furious rages.

"Leave everything to me," Fabian commanded. "According to the rules I either have to spirit you away tonight, which would be very uncomfortable, or if we leave very early tomorrow morning, which will be far more pleasant, we can be at my *Château* in Normandy early in the evening."

He paused before he added:

"We will be married there, by my Chaplain with no one to interfere."

"It sounds too .. perfect to be true."

"You are sure, you are absolutely sure that is what you want?"

"All I want," Loretta replied, "is for .. you to love me and .. even if I have .. as everybody will predict when they learn of our marriage .. only a very short time with you .. that will be better than a .. lifetime of misery and boredom .. with .. anyone else!"

She knew as she spoke she was being deliberately provocative, but Fabian's eyes were twinkling as he said:

"On our eightieth Wedding Anniversary you shall admit to me how wrong you were! All I can say is that you will find it very hard, my darling, to get rid of me, for I can no more lose you than lose half of my body and still be a living and breathing man."

There was a seriousness now in his last words that made Loretta move a little closer to him, and put her arms around his neck.

"Take me away .. please take me .. away," she begged. "I am so .. afraid this is all a .. wonderful dream and I shall .. wake up."

"And am I really your dream lover?"

"You know you are. You are .. everything that I ever .. wanted, but so much .. more that it is difficult to put into words how .. wonderful I think .. you are."

Fabian laughed and then he said:

"I would like you to try, but now, my precious, I want you to go back to the house and pack everything you want to bring with you and be ready when I collect you tomorrow morning at seven o'clock, if that is not too early."

"That is the time I usually go riding."

"We will ride when we are in Normandy."

"I have heard your horses are magnificent."

"You shall ride the very best of them, and I can only hope they will not disappoint you."

"Nothing can .. disappoint me .. now," Loretta said. "Oh, Fabian, is it really .. true that I am able to be your wife?"

"It is very much easier than if you had that mysterious husband lurking in the background!"

He was leading her across the lawn as he spoke, and when they reached the opening in the yew hedge he said:

"I am going to kiss you good-bye here."

"You do not .. want to stay .. here in the .. house?"

"I think that would be a mistake and, although it would perhaps be wise for you to inform your father whom you are marrying . . ."

He paused and smiled before he added:

"I shall leave mine in doubt. Although I am fond of him, he has obstinately refused to admit that I am grown-up and capable of running my life my own way."

Loretta gave a little cry of protest.

"We cannot start our .. married life by being unkind to anyone! I am so .. happy that I want the whole world to be happy .. too."

"You are right, my darling! That is what we will try to give to everyone we know, although – I am very sure that no one could be as happy as I am at this moment!"

"You do .. love me?" Loretta asked. "My running away as I .. did has not .. spoilt it for you?"

"It only tortured me into confessing to myself, what I already knew, that I cannot live without you. You are mine, mine completely, and my whole happiness depends on you."

"And my .. love will be .. enough?"

"Do you doubt that?"

"I love .. you with .. all of .. me," she whispered.

He kissed her gently before he said:

"You shall tell me about that tomorrow night when you are completely mine."

Then he was gone, walking away through the yew hedge.

Because she knew that he did not want her to follow him, she went back to the fountain.

She stood looking at the rainbows in the rise and fall of the water and felt that they were thrilling through her body.

Her happiness was too overwhelming to be expressed in words.

. . . . . . .

Afterwards Loretta could never remember how she spent the evening and the night before Fabian collected her.

She felt as if she was dancing on a rainbow underneath the stars, and it was impossible to think of anything mundane and matter-of-fact.

Somehow her trunks were packed, with Sarah grumbling because she had only just unpacked them.

Loretta sent a message to Cousin Emily to tell her that she was going away again the next morning.

She did not go to see her because Emily's lady's-maid said that she still had a very severe cold.

She had suggested when Loretta arrived home it would be a mistake to risk catching it, or the sore throat and bad cough which Emily was still suffering.

There were still two days before her father would return.

Loretta left a letter for him on his desk telling him briefly that she had met Fabian de Sauerdun by chance.

She told him that they had fallen in love with each other.

Because they both resented the idea of being pressurised into a marriage they had decided it was better to elope.

It was a very brief letter, but she ended it:

*"Please do not be angry, Papa. I know you love me and were doing what you thought was best for me, but now I am doing what I want and what I know is best for me. I am very, very happy.*

*Your affectionate and loving daughter,*
*Loretta."*

. . . . . . .

She was downstairs and waiting in the Hall when Fabian arrived at seven o'clock.

He was driving a very smart Phaeton, drawn by two horses.

She was to learn later he had borrowed them from the friend with whom he had stayed the night.

Following him was a brake drawn by six horses, in which travelled his valet with the luggage.

Fabian alighted from the Phaeton.

As Loretta moved towards him he looked into her eyes, raised her hand to his lips, and kissed it.

Without saying anything he helped her into the Phaeton.

They drove off with only the groom sitting behind them on a small seat.

Loretta knew that the servants were curious as to why she was leaving so early and who was collecting her.

It was only when they were half-way down the drive that she said half-teasingly:

"I wondered if perhaps during the night you had . . changed your . . mind!"

"I wondered the same thing," Fabian replied. "Then I knew, my courageous darling, that this was an adventure and something that you would enjoy in the same way that I will."

Loretta smiled at him and he said:

"We are going to make it even more difficult for those who will want to reproach us for doing them out of a smart, social wedding! We are to be married tonight in Normandy, but in two days' time, before our sins can catch up with us in the shape of our relatives, I am going to take you to North Africa."

Loretta gave a cry of delight.

"Do you really mean that? I thought that was .. reserved for .. Lady Brompton."

Fabian laughed.

"It is reserved for someone very beautiful who will be my wife! I have a great deal to show you, and there is a great deal for me to explore, not only in the desert, but also of you."

"I hope you will not be .. disappointed with what you .. find," Loretta said demurely.

"I think that is unlikely," Fabian answered.

Then he took one hand from the reins and laid it on hers as he said:

"My darling, only you could be brave enough to come away with me like this, and if you are regretting the absence of your trousseau, I promise you I will choose for you the most expensive and elaborate gowns any bride ever possessed!"

Loretta looked at him enquiringly, and he said with a twist on his lips:

"I am a Frenchman and, while no Englishman would bore himself by going to a dressmaker, I have every intention of deciding what you will or will not wear, and I will make you look even more beautiful than you are at the moment!"

"That will be fun," Loretta said. "Oh, Fabian, I am so happy!"

"And I am happy too," he replied. "I swear you will never regret marrying a man with the reputation of being a 'modern Casanova'."

"You know they call you that."

"Of course I know," he replied, "but I prefer to think

of myself as a Don Quixote, tilting at rainbows."

They drove on for a little while before he added:

"You know most men are really rather pathetic and very far from being as lucky as I am."

"What do you mean by that?"

"I told you when I met you it had been a long pilgrimage to find you, and I had met many disappointments. That is what every lover finds as he journeys through life, but is continually disappointed!"

His voice deepened as he said:

"Yet he goes on hoping that the next flower he picks from the roadside will be the perfection he is seeking, until it withers and he is forced to throw it away."

Loretta made an exclamation of horror.

"Suppose that . . happens to . . us?"

"Do you really think for a moment that it might?"

"You are quite . . sure it will . . not?"

"Absolutely and completely sure," Fabian replied. "I knew when you came into the Salon on that first night that my vibrations leapt towards you and you were encircled by a blinding light! You were what I had been waiting for and searching for."

"Did you really feel . . that? I felt your vibrations," Loretta said, "but I had been . . warned that every woman you met fell in love with you, and I was . . fighting against your . . attractiveness."

"I was certainly severely handicapped," Fabian said, "but despite all the problems and difficulties we have won, my darling, and tonight I will tell you how fortunate I am as I give you your first lesson in love."

"I shall be . . longing for . . that," Loretta whispered.

.   .   .   .   .   .   .

It was a long journey. They travelled first by train to Portsmouth where to Loretta's surprise Fabian's yacht was waiting for them in the harbour.

It was a new steam yacht that he had only

recently acquired.

Although the sea was calm he insisted that she went into the Master Cabin and rested while they crossed the Channel.

It was a large and very attractive cabin, and as he took her into it Fabian said:

"I am not going to show you now around my yacht, of which I am very proud, because we shall be using it again in two or three days' time when we leave our home – yours and mine, my precious – for North Africa."

"We are going by yacht? How exciting!"

"I hope you are a good sailor."

"I hope so too!" Loretta said. "It would be very unromantic to be sea-sick on my honeymoon."

Fabian laughed and kissed her.

Because she wanted to obey him, she lay down on the large comfortable bed and, which surprised her later, fell asleep.

She knew it was because she had lain awake for a long time the night before, feeling Fabian's kisses still on her lips.

The thrills of what he had said to her moving through her breasts.

Then she woke with a start as Fabian sat down on the bed and kissed her very gently.

"I was . . dreaming of . . you," she said drowsily.

"We have arrived, darling," he answered. "As we have nearly an hour's driving before we reach home, I want you now to get up."

"Of course," Loretta agreed, "and it will be very exciting to see your *Château*."

"*Our Château. Our* home," Fabian said quietly. "We will share it as we will share everything else."

. . . . . . .

Loretta saw the *Château* in front of them and once again thought she was dreaming.

They drove towards it in an open Phaeton drawn by

the finest and best bred horses she had ever seen.

Surrounded by trees it certainly looked like a dream Castle.

Its turrets and towers, the windows reflected the light of the late afternoon sun, the gardens were laid out in the traditional French fashion.

There was not one fountain, but five.

They were all playing and with the water falling into ornate stone basins they were even more magnificent than the one Fabian had taken her to see in the Bois.

The moment they arrived at the *Château*, Loretta wanted to look around and explore everything but Fabian insisted she went upstairs.

"We are getting married immediately," he said. "I can wait no longer for you to become my wife."

Loretta's eyes widened as she said:

"I thought you would . . arrange for it to be . . later."

She saw by the expression in his eyes how much he desired her but he said quietly:

"My Chaplain will be waiting for us as soon as you are ready. This Castle was my mother's when she was a girl, and you will find a veil which was worn by her when she married. I will also send you her tiara to wear with it. I want you, my precious one, to look like the bride who has always been in my dreams."

She flashed him a smile of sheer happiness.

She went up the stairs where she saw a Housekeeper in rustling black, waiting for her at the top of the stairs.

She was a grey-haired woman, and as she took Loretta along the corridor she said:

"This is a very happy day for all of us, *Mademoiselle*. We have prayed and prayed that *Monsieur le Marquis* would marry, and now that I see you I know you are exactly what *Madame*, his mother, whom we all loved, would have chosen for him."

"Thank you," Loretta smiled.

The room into which she was shown, and which she knew had been Fabian's mother's, she found very beautiful.

The painted ceiling depicted Venus surrounded by cupids rising from the sea.

The huge four-poster bed had a canopy carved with gold cupids carrying garlands of flowers.

Loretta had instructed Sarah to put in with her gowns one that had been sent down from London for her to wear when she made her curtsy at Buckingham Palace.

It was white with a bustle of chiffon frills and the chiffon which encircled the décolletage was sprinkled with diamanté.

It made her think it looked like the drops of water falling into the fountains.

She covered her fair hair and her face with the fine Brussels lace veil which reached down to the floor.

When the maids who were attending her set the beautiful tiara shaped like a wreath of flowers on her head, she knew she not only looked like a bride, but also a little like the goddess from Olympus Fabian thought her to be.

She was told he was waiting for her downstairs.

A bouquet had been handed into the bedroom consisting of white roses and lilies-of-the-valley.

Loretta knew it was symbolic of the purity that Fabian found in her.

She blushed a little as she thought of it.

Then as she went down the stairs and saw him waiting for her in the Hall she knew no man in the whole world could look so handsome or so irresistibly attractive.

He was wearing full evening-dress which she was aware was customary in France.

It was the first time she had seen his decorations.

She resolved that one day soon she would ask him why he had received them. She was certain some were for gallantry.

He watched her come slowly down towards him.

When he met her as she reached the bottom step he said very softly:

"No woman could look so perfect! I know, Heart of my Heart, that you are an angel come to me from Heaven!"

She smiled at him beneath her veil and he put her arm through his and drew her down a long corridor away from the centre of the *Château*.

She guessed the Chapel would be on the East side.

As they neared it there was the soft sound of organ music.

But when they entered Loretta could only see the Chaplain waiting for them at the Altar.

There were two servers on either side of him.

It was a very short service as Loretta was not a Roman Catholic.

As they knelt and they were blessed, she told herself that she would become one so that she could worship with Fabian and with their children when they had them.

The little Chapel did not seem to her empty as she rose for Fabian to lead her away from the Altar.

She felt that the faith of those who had worshipped here over many centuries was vivid and inescapable.

There was no need for a living congregation to wish them happiness.

To Loretta's surprise they did not go, as she had expected, into a Salon and toast each other in champagne.

Instead Fabian took her up the stairs and into another bedroom which she thought must connect with hers.

It was larger, just as beautiful, but more magnificent with a painted ceiling and antique furniture that must have escaped the Revolution.

There was a huge bed draped with crimson curtains and embroidered with Fabian's coat of arms under a canopy, so exquisitely carved and gilded that Loretta wanted to inspect it more closely.

But it was impossible for her to have eyes for anything but her husband.

He shut the door and drew her across the room to the window so that she could look out at the fountains playing in the flower-filled garden.

"This is your home, my precious," he said, "and I want you to love it as I do, and to make it a place of love for everyone who lives in it."

"That is what I .. want to .. do."

Then she moved closer to him as she asked:

"Are we really .. married? Am I really your .. wife? I was sure when you were .. angry with me you did not .. want me .. any more."

"You are my wife," Fabian said in a deep voice, "and I intend to prove it, my darling one, so that it is something you will never doubt again."

As he spoke he very gently lifted the tiara from her head and after it the lace veil.

He put them both down on an adjacent chair and drew her close to him.

Tipping up her chin he kissed her at first very tenderly as if she were infinitely precious.

Then, as he felt her quiver with the excitement and rapture he always evoked in her, his kisses became more passionate, more demanding.

As she felt as if once again she was dancing on a rainbow up into the sky she felt her gown slither from her body down onto the floor.

Then as Fabian lifted her up into his arms she gave a little exclamation of surprise.

As he carried her towards the bed he said:

"*Cinq-a-Sept* in France is a time for rest, and because I am teaching you French customs, my adorable one, that is a polite way of saying I want to love you."

He put her down against the soft, lace-trimmed pillows, and as she lay there she was sure that once again she was dreaming.

When she woke up the Château and its fountains would

have vanished and she would find her dream lover had only been a figment of her imagination.

Then Fabian was beside her, and as she felt him pull her into his arms, she knew that it was real – she had found him and she was his wife.

She felt then as if the love that had moved like sunshine in her body all day seemed to intensify.

It swept her like a tidal wave towards him, closer and closer until she felt as his heart beat against hers, they were one person and indivisible.

"My precious, my darling, my perfect and adorable little wife!" Fabian said in a deep voice. "You are mine and we have escaped not only from our fathers, but from the world and from everything that is ugly and unpleasant."

He pulled her closer as he went on:

"We are starting a new life, you and I, and our love will show us the way to a happiness which may seem incredible, but which I know is ours for eternity."

"I . . love you . . I love . . you, Fabian," Loretta whispered.

She felt him kiss her lips, her neck, her breasts.

His vibrations captured and imprisoned hers until she had no identity of her own.

She was a part of him, and a rainbow was carrying her higher and higher up into the sky.

Flashing through her body it turned into little flames of passion which joined with the flaming fire in Fabian.

She could feel the heat of it consuming her until she could no longer think, but only feel . . and feel . . .

"This is . . love! Oh . . Fabian . . I love . . you!"

"You are mine – my darling – my perfect little goddess – my wife. Give yourself to me."

"I am . . yours . . all . . yours!"

Then as the rainbow touched the stars above them and the rapture became an ecstasy which was almost a pain in its intensity, Fabian made Loretta his.

Coming next in your collection of
The Romantic Novels of
BARBARA CARTLAND

# FORCED TO MARRY

Gytha is told by her grandfather, the wealthy
Sir Robert Sullivan, that because she is his heir,
she is to marry one of his nephews. She thinks
both are repulsive and searches frantically for
some escape.

She learns that her father when at War with
Napoleon, saved the life of their neighbour, the
fashionable and magnificent Lord Locke, with
whom her grandfather is not on speaking
terms. Desperately she goes to Lord Locke for
help.

How His Lordship uses Gytha to free him
from the clutching hands of Princess Zuleika,
and how they both encounter danger and dis-
aster is told in this thrilling new novel by Barbara Cartland.